PLAY IT BACK

VANESSA LOPEZ AZIZ

NewLink Publishing

2023

Play it Back
Vanessa Lopez Aziz
Copyright © 2023
All rights reserved

Copy Editor: Sarah Albrecht
Interior Design: Jo A Wilkins
Cover Design: Vanessa Aziz & Janelle Evans

1. Young Adult Fiction/Science Fiction/General
2. Fiction/Science Fiction/Time Travel
3. Young Adult Fiction/Coming of Age

ISBN: 978-1-948266-85-7 Trade Paperback
ISBN: 978-1-948266-99-7 E-Book

www.iqpublishers.com
Henderson, NV

Published and Printed in the United States of America

1 2 3 4 5 6 7 8 9 10

Dedication

I'd like to dedicate this book to the three people who had to share my time and energy with this novel — my husband Tom and my children Lincoln and Luna. Sorry for all the late nights and constant distraction.

Second, I'd like to dedicate this story to my own Lola. Thank you for telling me your stories and seeing me. Not just the version of me others told you about me, but the unique flawed human I am.

Last, I'd like to dedicate this story to all the other nerds, whose adolescence was both analog and digital, who were awkward and weird and shy and who found community in small pockets of fandom growing all over the web in the late 90s. Look, all that dorky stuff is cool now. Just ask Gen Z! Current fashion looks ripped straight out of my high school closet circa 2003. The internet does not have to divide us. For me, it was a place I could go to find my people.

Author Note

In this novel, I use Tagalog interspersed with English and American Sign Language. Carmen's family is from Pampanga, and the local dialect is Kapampangan. Most Filipino people I know speak their local dialect at home and use Tagalog for official reasons like school and television. For simplicity's sake, I chose to stick with Tagalog, the national language, where possible.

The grammar structure of American Sign Language is quite different from spoken English. As a visual language, ASL relies heavily on facial expressions as much as signs to communicate. For ease of reading, I translated the signs to English grammar and syntax, instead of directly from the signs.

Glossary of Terms

- **Anak:** Term of endearment for a child
- **Apo:** Grandchild
- **Haynako:** Oh my gosh. An expression of disgust, annoyance, or surprise
- **Kumusta:** Hello
- **Lola:** Grandmother
- **Nanay:** Mother
- **Pancit:** Popular Filipino noodle dish
- **Parol:** Star-shaped lanterns that represent the north star and are popular Christmas decorations in the Philippines.
- **Sinigang:** Filipino sour tamarind soup
- **Susmaryosep:** A word blend of Jesus, Mary, and Joseph. Used as a term of exclamation, like hay nako.
- **Tagalog:** The official language of the Philippines. There are between 120-187 dialects spoken in the Philippines, depending on the method of classification.
- **Tatay:** Father

ACT ONE

A frequently said proverb in Tagalog is—

Ang hindi marunong lumingon sa pinanggalingan ay hindi makakarating sa paroroonan.

Roughly translated, this means—

A person who doesn't know how to look back to where he came from, won't reach his destination.

CHAPTER 1

The dreaded high school reunion occupied Jamboree High's basketball gym. Cheap streamers and flimsy foil curtains decorated the doorways, and a small disco ball hung limply from each hoop. If the theme was "sad," they hit the mark.

To continue the pattern, a funeral wreath rested in the entryway. It displayed a photo of Mrs. Malone, the teacher who died during Carmen's senior year in high school. Carmen never took any of Mrs. Malone's classes but knew that she died while running with the cross-country team. Her death cast a shadow over their end-of-year festivities with moments of silence at prom and graduation. Students cried in the halls and the theater and cross-country students erected a veritable shrine near the drama room she'd taught in for fifteen years.

Mrs. Malone's teenage daughter sat in a wheelchair by the wreath, greeting former students as they entered. She used sign language to communicate with an older man standing next to her, the widower of said teacher. Although fluent in sign language, Carmen didn't have

1

any memories to share, so she veered toward the stage to find a table.

Logan stood on the wooden platform, tuning his guitar, and preparing to play with his former high school band. He gave her a wide smile when he spotted her watching him. His canines were a little too long and sat forward from the rest of his teeth, like a fox or the vampire in every story she secretly loved.

It was this smile that won her over a year ago when they ran into each other at a music festival. She had been separated from her group, slightly tipsy, and texting her missing friends when someone called her name. She turned to find an attractive but unfamiliar man looking at her, head tilted. He had a five o'clock shadow and long hair gathered in a bun at the base of his neck.

"Carmen?"

"Yes?" She hoped this wasn't someone she'd treated at the hospital. She hated running into former patients, especially while out drinking.

"Did you go to Jamboree High?"

"Yes...?" She stretched the word out in question.

"Logan Sardino. We graduated the same year."

"Wow, hi! Yeah, I remember you. Sort of. I'm surprised you remember me."

She remembered Logan, but only in that distant way popular guys stood out in memory. It wasn't his face so much as the idea of him she remembered, as the lead in every play and breezing through the halls with a crowd of his fellow jocks. If their high school social circles were a Venn diagram, there would be no Venn to diagram. They hardly knew each other.

Gesturing to her voluminous hair, made thicker by the damp air, he huffed a laugh. "It's the hair. It's distinctive."

Reflexively, she brushed said mane back from her face. "Yeah, people called me—"

"Ramen, I remember," he said.

She gained the moniker in a schoolyard scuffle in the fourth grade. Some kids started a chant of "Jingle bells, Ramen smells" when she'd brought leftover pancit—a popular Filipino noodle dish full of liver and shrimp—to lunch. She'd started to cry until two girls dumped their food trays over the singers' heads. This prompted an all-out food fight that earned them all detention. Those two strangers later became Carmen's lifelong friends, Josie and Ganesha.

As if Carmen's thoughts called her over, Ganesha nudged her in greeting, breaking her out of her reminiscing.

Ganesha's tailored suit was made of velvet, and she had pink extensions braided into her thick black hair. She'd fully embraced fashion in college and wore progressively more Instagram-able outfits the older she grew. A far cry from the standard jeans and oversized T-shirt combo she'd worn to blend in during high school.

"Look at you, dating the prom king." Ganesha gestured toward the stage. "I would never have imagined it."

Carmen rolled her eyes. "Please don't remind me. I try to forget what a betrayal it is to my childhood self."

Josie and her husband Mark followed Ganesha over, hugging Carmen in greeting. Josie's rich blonde hair glowed bronze in the reflected fairy lights, hanging down rather than pulled back in the perpetual messy ponytail she hadn't bothered to change since grade school. Her hand rested protectively over her baby bump, just starting to show. Josie would be the first of her friends to have a baby to fuss over. Carmen looked forward to spoiling the child rotten.

"I'm honestly shocked we all came," Ganesha said. "I blame that boyfriend of yours, Ramen. Come on." She linked arms with them both. "Let's show these losers what success looks like."

An hour or so later, they were surrounded by classmates due to the flasks of rum Ganesha and Carmen snuck into the supposedly alcohol-free event.

Impressed, Carmen watched her former wallflower friend, Ganesha, flirt with an ex-cheerleader who clearly returned the interest. Brittany or Chelsea or Kelly? Carmen hadn't caught her name. Ganesha's overly traditional Indian family hadn't approved of her coming out during college, but they did eventually come around.

While Ganesha and the cheerleader bonded over travel and poli-sci, the usually reserved Josie attracted a crowd of fellow law graduates, exchanging exam stories like war veterans.

As more rum made its way into the group's plastic cups, Josie consoled a teary-eyed guy who recently failed the Bar Exam.

"Honestly, Adam, the Bar Exam is tough, especially the California Bar. Failing the first time is practically expected!"

"Did you?"

"Um, no, but you went to a much better law school than I did," the blonde said with false cheer. She patted his shoulder. "I'm sure you'll pass next time."

Were those tears in his eyes? Maybe it was time to stop being so generous with the flask.

"Next time." He sniffed. "Thank you. Hey, did we have any classes together? I'm surprised we weren't

4

friends back then."

Counting on her fingers, Josie named them. "We had AP History together. And AP Physics. And AP Government. And AP English."

"That can't be right! I'm sure I'd have remembered you..."

At Josie's shrug, Carmen rescued her from having to say more.

"I heard an interesting story about your car." She gave him a sly grin.

He scratched the back of his neck, looking chagrined. "Yeah... I was kind of an idiot. My parents were angels, honestly. I should have been cut off and forced to take the bus."

He had driven his expensive sports car onto the high school football field as a prank during the year's final game, then ran across the area, naked. He recounted the story with some reluctance when Josie asked.

"My parents paid the school some crazy amount of money to fix the damage. And to stop them from expelling me." His cheeks flushed from either the whiskey or, more likely, embarrassment.

"That was you?" Josie said. "I kind of remember hearing about that."

"Yeah... I was dared to by some of the guys on the team." He shrugged as if this was an adequate explanation.

"Hmm." Josie's sound contained both disappointment and judgment. She already sounded like a mom.

"I'm lucky I didn't get into more trouble. But you know, when else could I have done something so crazy? High school was so much fun."

Many of their former classmates had lived charmed

lives, with little responsibility and unlimited funds. Not so for kids like Carmen and her friends. Coming from low-income families in a school full of rich kids likely pushed them to become such close friends in their formative years. They hadn't partied, they didn't drink, they didn't date. They couldn't afford the kind of frivolity Adam had engaged in.

"It sounds like it was a good time," Carmen said, vaguely.

He pivoted from Josie to Carmen. "So, you're here with the Loginator, huh?"

"Yeah." She prevented an eye roll in the nickname, just barely. Logan's band finished their last song to a round of applause.

"Cool. What high school did you go to?"

She furrowed her eyebrows. "This one?"

"You did?" He looked just as perplexed.

"Yeah."

Scratching his head, he said, "Were you guys dating then?"

"No. We ran into each other a year ago."

"What a small world," he said. "You guys went to high school together but didn't know each other, only to date ten years later?"

"That about covers it."

She'd had some version of this conversation with several classmates tonight. People thought she was Logan's plus-one rather than a fellow reunion attendee. Everyone knew Logan. In high school he'd straddled several cliques—the smart kids because of his stellar grades, the jocks because of water polo, and the artsy types due to theater. Carmen only had two friends from high school. Apparently, they were the only two who remembered her. It was funny the first or second time, but now it was becoming ridiculous. Carmen had taken classes with Adam.

Sharply gesturing hands distracted Carmen, and she turned to see the widower signing to his daughter.

"Do you need..." Something something, "... tired?" The man signed. The distance made it hard to see the nuances.

More signing. "Only dizzy."

"Okay..." Something. "... no."

Logan nudged her. "Hey, want to slow dance? I love this song."

With Logan's set done and his gear packed away, a radio station of hits played through the speakers. They went out on the dance floor, the music soft and slow. She burrowed into his neck as they swayed with the rhythm, breathing in his scent. Like grass and spiced tea. And a little like mothballs. His velvet jacket needed a wash.

"You look pretty spectacular tonight."

"Thank you! I dressed to impress."

"You made an impression on me." He ran his hands through her hair. "I'm so glad this puff of fluff was blocking my view of that stage last year, or I never would have spotted you."

"Puff of fluff?" She batted his hand away.

"What? It's puffy and fluffy, just like a cloud. Or like a lion."

His obsession with her hair both charmed and annoyed her. "You're lucky you're cute because you do *not* have a way with words."

"A beautiful lion? A *fierce* lion." He bared his misaligned canines at her.

She laughed, nestling back into him as they danced.

The song changed, and Carmen recognized the opening notes. It was their song. An old classic done and redone over the years. The same version that played the day they met. The raw, throaty voice gave the lyrics substance and never failed to tug at something deep in her chest.

"Lucky to have her,
Lucky, she has you.
With a winning hand at poker,
I'd still bet on you.
If I walked by a four-leaf clover,
I'd always pick you.
I'd choose a life sober,
than a day without you..."

Pulled in for a kiss, the rasp of his facial hair sent electricity down her gut like always. He withdrew from the kiss to look at her, his expression intense. The slant of his eyebrows held a question.

"Damn," he said as he came to some internal decision. He knelt on one knee without breaking eye contact and brought a small wooden box out of his pocket. Inside, nestled between velvet folds, sat a simple ring with a green peridot, her birthstone.

"Tomorrow is your birthday, and I was going to propose at dinner with your friends and family, but this song is perfect, and this moment is perfect, and honey, you're perfect. I can't wait another day to ask you. Carmen, will you marry me?"

She stood dumbstruck. They hadn't even discussed marriage. She loved him, but they'd barely shared a lease for two months. Did he want kids? Did she want kids? Oh, God. She thought she knew him, but did she? There were so many people around. Ganesha and Josie smiled excitedly. Had they known? His friends clapped while Paul pulled out a phone to take photos. And was someone yelling?

"Help! Someone call 911!"

The chaos turned the crowd away from the spectacle of Logan's proposal. Even Logan, whose smile faded at her prolonged hesitation, looked toward the commotion.

The music cut out.

Feeling both grateful and guilty for her relief at the distraction, Carmen stepped toward the call for help. "I'm a nurse, what's going on?"

The crowd parted. The teenage girl in the wheelchair seized violently, sliding down in her seat as the older gentleman attempted to pull her up.

"She's choking!" He gasped.

Pushing through the last of the stunned crowd, Carmen assessed the scene. "Is this her first seizure?"

"No, but she was eating when it started. I think she's choking!"

Her face looked waxy, and Carmen observed no gasping or wheezing through the quaking.

Free of the crowd, she rushed to the wheelchair, giving the older gentleman orders as she did so. "Pull her up under her arms. I'll pull the chair away to do the Heimlich. Help me hold her up. And watch her face. She'll likely vomit."

The wheelchair was hauled away as her father propped the shaking girl up. Carmen brought her arms around to her front, sharply bringing her now joined fists to the girl's abdomen and up.

She thrust once, twice, and on the third, the girl spit

9

out food and vomited. She threw her head back sharply, hitting the bridge of Carmen's nose and forehead with a crack. Stars burst in Carmen's vision. Pain exploded at the point of contact, and she let go.

The widower caught the girl's full weight as Carmen stumbled to the ground. Her nose freely bled down her face. The room spun, and she felt sick. Logan crouched at her side. "Are you okay?"

Coughing up blood, she failed to answer.

The room tunneled as she fell.

CHAPTER 2

In a flat green field beneath moving diaphanous clouds in a neon blue sky, Carmen lay sprawled. In the distance, a treehouse perched in a lone tree. The cartoonish structure squatted between three prongs of a great oak. Wooden shutters bracketed the solitary window, underscored with a line of flowerpots.

Pushing herself up from her prone position, she walked toward it.

The grass felt good under her feet, crisp and wet. Between one blink and the next, the tree loomed above her, and she climbed the ladder hammered to the trunk. When she pushed the floor plank up to look inside the little house, the choking girl in the wheelchair sat in front of the window.

The girl signed to Carmen. "I'd always wanted to climb this treehouse."

"I'm Carmen." Rapidly moving her hands to spell her name first, she gave her sign name, the letter C and the sign for noodles combined. She'd taken sign language through high school and college, and her deaf college professor gave her the name. Deaf culture gave unique signs to people in their community, which often combined physical or personality traits with letters. People noticed the distinctive curl of her hair before all else.

The deaf girl watched her sign but didn't respond directly, continuing her train of thought. "You know what else I wanted? More time with my mom. She died when I was seven." She paused for a moment to look out at the green expanse.

Studying her profile, Carmen searched for some response to that statement.

Abruptly, the deaf girl turned, her intense blue eyes boring into her own. "What do you want?"

Carmen flinched. The question gave her the same paralyzing anxiety Logan's question had. Because what *did* she want?

Blinking, Carmen woke up somewhere both familiar and utterly disorienting. She must have hit her head harder than she thought. Sunlight poured through the open window, piercing her from eye to temple. Squinting at the ceiling for a moment, she let her eyes adjust. Photo and magazine cutouts cluttered one wall. A clunky computer monitor took up much of the desk. She recognized the damaged blinds, the collage wall, and the pile of clothes spilling out of the half-open closet.

Her childhood bedroom! This made no sense. Her parents sold the place years ago.

What was going on? She jumped out of bed but sat back down when the room spun around her. Standing slowly this time to accommodate her pounding head, she staggered to the collection of taped-up photos for a closer look. There she was with Josie and Ganesha at the chain bookstore in town, at the boardwalk, at concerts, perched on the swings at the neighborhood park.

An accumulation of pre-college detritus papered the walls. It had all been packed away a month after graduation and carted from apartment to apartment for years. She still possessed some of the photos, but most were lost to time or uploaded to the cloud years ago.

In the mirror, she caught sight of herself and gaped at the changed person it presented. Above stunned eyes sat overplucked eyebrows, a broad forehead scattered with pubescent acne, and the same thick curly hair cut shorter than adult Carmen preferred. Her gangly coltish legs wobbled, wrongfooted in this body. She pinched herself. It didn't hurt, so she squeezed harder. Ow. That hurt.

Another scan of the walls showed no handy calendar to check the date. With a flash of inspiration, Carmen remembered she religiously kept a journal for years. That should give her an idea of when she was. Where had she hidden them? Under the bed? No… At the top of her closet? Not there either. She unearthed a dusty shoebox from the back of her closet full of well-worn journals. The bubbly script and content screamed middle school. Mirror Carmen did not look like a middle schooler.

Carmen turned to her desk with another flash of insight, recalling that her journal migrated from paper to the internet around her sophomore year. The boxy beige computer looked ancient to Carmen's eyes. Navigating to the bottom right-hand corner of the pixelated screen, the date blinked stark and green.

August 23, 1999. NINETEEN NINETY-NINE.

She was seventeen years old today. Panic seized her. A barrage of contradictory sensations roiled through her. Hot, cold, nauseated, dizzy. Had she died and gone to purgatory? Her stomach churned like curtled milk. Why did all this feel like reality when it couldn't be?

She had planned on suffering through her high school reunion, then sleeping with Logan and waking up the following day twenty-seven years old. Instead, she woke up *seventeen*.

At the worst or best possible moment, when dread rose like a flood she would drown in, her door opened.

"Anak! Get up. You have to... Oh! You're awake already? You didn't stay up all night on that computer, did you?"

Her mom.

Carmen had seen her yesterday. She had looked worn out, gray roots showing, a parenthesis between bunched brows with deep frown lines that bracketed downturned lips. The antithesis of that exhausted version stood before her, with subtle, flattering makeup and sleek bob, hair a perfect uniform black. She was young and vibrating with energy.

Her mom's rapid commentary continued without input from Carmen who remained static with surprise.

"I have to go to the store, and I know you need some school supplies, so get ready. I'm going soon, and I'm not going to wait for you. If you're not ready in half an hour, I'm leaving without you."

No. She couldn't spend the day driving around in the car with her mom. Spending time with her tried her patience on a good day. Not to mention the disaster Carmen would be with no context for the current time.

"Mom, I feel sick, and my stomach hurts." She bent over, holding her stomach in emphatic distress. "I think I'm coming down with something."

"*Aye*, you stay up all night drawing or on your

14

computer. *Pah*, it's too much. You're making yourself sick. And what is all that reading doing? Your grades last year were terrible. You're not stupid. If you're staying home, clean your room."

And she was gone. Her mom was like the Energizer bunny if the Energizer bunny was a nagging Asian woman fueled by coffee and rice.

The reminder about her computer brought Carmen back to her desktop. She had a blog on an online community called LyfeJournal and poured hours of her life reading fanfiction on the same site. Carmen's interests mostly centered around science fiction and fantasy. She had a modest following, drawing scenes from her favorites in comic book style.

Her online alter-ego @missAnthropic was outgoing, talented, and popular, at least among the faceless friends she made online. Embarrassed, she never told Josie and Ganesha about her thriving online community and didn't carry the habit far into her post-high school life. Once the grind of college, work, and responsibilities caught up with her, she lacked the spare time to devote to hobbies.

She navigated to the internet and waited through the harsh low tones and beeps of dial-up before her computer connected. She'd left her LyfeJournal account logged in, and the previous day's entry presented itself first.

"I never thought I'd say this, but I am looking forward to school starting next week. I am SO tired of being around the house. My mom is driving me CRAZY. I cannot stand that woman. Does she know how miserable she makes everyone around her? If I have to listen to any more running commentary about how disappointed my mom is in me, I will run away.

"Seriously. I'll join a circus. I'll board a train! Do people even hobo like that anymore? I don't have any gross deformities or unique talents. Hmmm. Let's put a pin in that idea to mull over later. I think there is potential.

"Anyway, I'm making progress on the cover art for @BearyFunny's submission to Bookstafaria. She let me read a work-in-progress of her story, and I promise you guys will love it when she posts it."

Carmen had spent more time reading and drawing than getting any actual schoolwork done. Funny that she was such a slacker in her teen years when adult Carmen rarely took a day off from work, leaving her hobbies behind like this house.

"I will be SEVENTEEN tomorrow, which is insane. The last year of my childhood. G and J are picking me up tonight, and we're going to get burgers by the beach, then see a movie. Summer movies are never good, but I just love going to the movies. I love popcorn, I love ICEE's..."

She'd also liked the guy who worked at the concession stand.

> "I don't have a shift at The Hole until Saturday, so I'll have plenty of time to catch up on your cover art @ BearyFunny, I promise."

The HollyJolly was a chain restaurant she worked at during her last two years of high school. She aptly dubbed it "The Hole" on her blog, lest she be called out by some corporate HollyJolly spy and sued for libel.

Reaching the end of her most recent journal entry, the enormity of her situation swamped her again. Maybe if she went to sleep, she would wake up an adult and this nightmare would be over. Carmen logged off her blog with a passing notion to keep her private writing from her prying mom and climbed back into bed. Her heart beat too fast, she had to pee, and hunger gnawed at her stomach, but she shut her eyes anyway. Long minutes passed, and the churning in her stomach and brain began to slow when her mom barged back in.

"Don't think I've forgotten." She clearly had. "Happy Birthday! Oh! Are you back in bed? Okay, if you're not feeling well, get some rest. I'll leave some money out for you and your dad to get some pizza for lunch."

Her mom patted her feet under the blanket as she left the room.

There went the bit of calm she'd achieved. Instead, her newly agitated thoughts vacillated between past and future, trying to make sense of her situation.

That poor girl — she hadn't caught her name — suffered a seizure and choked. In the chaos, she'd headbutted

Carmen into some sort of…weird dream or hallucination where they talked in a treehouse?

Like all dreams, the edges were fuzzy and faded, and she only recalled bits and pieces.

The field. The treehouse. The girl and her wish to spend more time with her mom.

Did that mean Carmen should find a way to save the mom? Give her a future where she lived? How was she supposed to do that? Should she even try meddling? Messing with the future, the future where Carmen was happy, seemed like a poor choice to make. But then, why was she here, now? The teacher's death and her dream seemed to point to some greater purpose.

From what she remembered Mrs. Malone had died of a stroke. How did one prevent a stroke? As a nurse, she knew the medical recommendations—keep blood pressure low, eat a healthy diet, and exercise. But it wasn't like avoiding a car accident, and Carmen couldn't just stop the woman from getting into a car that day. No magical fix existed for a stroke. What was she going to do, smack a burger out of her hands? The woman ran cross-country, for goodness' sake! She knew all too well that bad things happened to good people all the time.

What do you want? The girl had asked her in the dream. The simple question triggered an incongruous wash of fear, a sensation like waking from a night terror, heart-stopping and terrible.

Logan! The impossible series of events that led Carmen to her childhood room in 1999 had briefly overshadowed the proposal. She loved Logan, but marriage? She didn't know if she could love him forever. Tying herself to anyone or anything gave her another flush of apprehension. Was it normal to fear commitment this much? She loved Logan, but the idea of marriage terrified her. A younger version of Logan existed here, too, about to start his senior year, completely unaware of her as a person. Was she here to...answer her question about what she wanted?

Was there a reason she was here at all?

It all seemed far-fetched, but she was in the past somehow with knowledge of the future. How could this be her reality and not some fever dream? She pinched herself again, but all it did was leave a red welt. There was no waking up from this nightmare.

CHAPTER 3

She didn't fall asleep. Eventually, she got up and returned to her blog, trying to gain more information. She drew fan art of some of the books and movie characters she liked. There were cartoon strips uploaded, funny little four to six-panel cartoons that made her laugh. She also found comments from old internet friends.

@Archimedes commented on her entry from the previous night.

> "Happy Birthday @missAnthropic! I hope you have a good one! I'm sorry about your mom. My mom still hopes I'll bring home a girl to shower her with grandchildren. Hah! Good luck with that. As a gift, I recommend reading the most recent chapter of my story. I put in a little Easter egg for you."

@BearyFunny wrote…

> "Girl, you are too good to me! Happy
> birthday! I sent you a little something
> via snail mail."

@BearyFunny, AKA Francis, was the only online friend she shared authentic details with, such as her real name, phone number, and address. Francis was a mid-30s mother who lived on the East Coast, so the possibility of gaining a stalker was low risk.

@BearyFunny's writing, both fanfiction and original fiction was quality work. She would eventually publish dozens of romance novels, but at this time, she was strictly a fanfiction writer. Carmen preferred supporting her online community by drawing or editing for other people and rarely wrote her own stories.

Sudden inspiration struck her. She started a new blog entry.

> "Hey guys! Thanks so much for
> the birthday well-wishes! I really
> appreciate it. I'm looking forward to
> celebrating tonight.
>
> "Could I get opinions from you
> guys? I'm thinking about drawing
> a comic book story involving time
> travel. I know, it's such a fanfiction
> trope, but there's a reason it's a
> trope. Who doesn't want to go back
> and fix something or save someone?
> I know time-travel stories get pretty

complicated and plot holes are difficult to avoid. The story is set up with the main character thrown back to their old body, so there is no double to avoid. They have all the knowledge of the future, but no idea how to get back. Here are some of the issues I'm concerned with...

1. What happens if the character changes something?
2. Can they erase their future?
3. Will time and space collapse if things are changed?"

Maybe she was being dramatic, but she was genuinely worried. Who better to ask than the collective hive mind of a bunch of science fiction writers about her very sci-fi situation? But in all the stories she read, the characters always seemed to know what to do. She felt paralyzed. She had indigestion from all the existential dread. A solid meal would be her reward for abandoning the relative safety of her bedroom.

The half-forgotten but common sight of her dad sleeping on the Lazy-Boy greeted her as she came downstairs. Her dad never slept in the bedroom. Instead, he preferred a half-reclined position, which relieved pressure from a construction workplace injury that put him on disability with constant back pain.

The pizza money her mom promised sat next to the phone. Finding a well-worn menu stuck to the fridge, Carmen called and placed an order.

Dad woke as she hung up.

"Anak? Happy birthday! How are you feeling?" His Filipino accent was present but less pronounced than her mom's.

"Fine? Oh! Yeah, my stomach is all better." Carmen recalled her excuse now. "I think I just needed a little more sleep."

"Good. Did you get pepperoni and pineapple?"

"Of course."

"Good girl. Can you help me find the remote? I can't watch anymore of this." He gestured toward the TV where the news droned on at low volume.

Perusing the TV guide, they settled on old I Love Lucy episodes. Soon, they ate the delivery pizza and snickered alongside the laugh tracks that accompanied their peanut-gallery commentary. Carmen especially appreciated the clothing.

"How about I just start dressing like I Love Lucy for school? Poodle skirts and coiffed hair. I could pull it off!"

"I support this decision. It's timeless."

"It really isn't. But maybe for Halloween?"

"I thought you were too old for dressing up?"

Carmen loved Halloween. Did she stop dressing up in high school? She couldn't remember.

"No one is too old for Halloween. Maybe we could convince Mom to do a family costume this year. One last hurrah before college."

Her dad just gave her a look. They'd never done a family costume.

"Hey." Noticing the time, she stood. "Speaking of clothes, I've gotta get ready. I think Ganesha and Josie will be by soon to pick me up."

Her dad sat up, then winced. He reached into his pocket for his ever-present oxycodone.

"Dad, cool it with the pills, okay?"

The grimace she saw from him made her regret the words almost as soon as they left her. She never nagged him about the medication because her mom said enough about it for them both.

Her dad never took more than was strictly recommended by the pain doctor. Unfortunately, he was entirely reliant on them to function. He took two pills every four hours, like clockwork, night or day.

"I promise, after this next surgery, I should be able to take less."

After the subsequent surgery, she knew he would take more. His dependence on them and their financial ruin would lead to her parents' divorce. The failure of his marriage would spur him to quit and quit for good.

In her present time, her dad worked as a truck driver, had a new girlfriend, and lived near Carmen. They saw each other every Sunday night. It was a good life. But she felt powerless right then to do anything for him.

"Love you, Dad," she said, then hugged him as a kind of silent apology and went upstairs to get ready.

Looking through her closet brought nothing but despair. All she owned were cargo pants, ill-fitting jeans, band T-shirts, and hoodies. She liked the band T-shirts, but they were enormous, like she'd intended to use them for an emergency shelter rather than wear them like actual clothes. And ugh, low-rise jeans. Why had anyone thought those were a good idea? Horrible. Horrible. Horrible.

'90s fashion was fun! Grunge, spaghetti straps, daisy chains, and platform shoes were all acceptable period fashion she could get behind. Why had she refused to participate? High school Carmen dressed like a middle-aged dad.

At the back of the closet, she found a white eyelet dress with the tags still on. She assumed her mom purchased it for her. Remembering her mom's full closet, she also raided it and unearthed a leather jacket she didn't plan to give back. She put it on and was satisfied overall. It was nothing close to what she would have worn in high school, but she felt physically incapable of putting on cargo pants. They were hideous—no wonder she hadn't dated until college.

She looked at herself in the mirror one last time, then turned to go as she heard the doorbell ring. This outfit was very generation appropriate anyway. No one would make a big deal out of it.

CHAPTER 4

"You're wearing a dress? Did your mom make you wear it?"

Apparently, Ganesha would make a big deal out of it. Unlike the long wavy black hair and pink extensions of adult Ganesha, teen Ganesha's hair was cut in a severe bob and blow-dried straight, her only attempt at vanity at this age. Otherwise, she was swamped by an oversized gray sweater and bland jeans.

"Hello to you too."

"Hi, happy birthday. What are you wearing?"

"Clothes! Let's go."

Carmen stepped past Ganesha onto the pathway leading to the parking lot. After a few steps, she realized that she didn't remember which car to walk to and let Ganesha take the lead. Luckily, Josie's hell on wheels waited at the curb. It was uglier than she recalled but wholly recognizable. The old beater stalled at stop lights, stank of old cigarettes, and the dash was forever lit with various warning lights. But it was Josie's pride and joy.

"Happy birthday!" Josie smiled and waved to her from the driver's seat. "Did your mom make you wear that?" She looked mostly the same as her adult version, except without the baby bump. She looked especially tiny behind the driver's wheel, with the seat pulled up as close as it could get to reach the pedals.

"Everyone's a critic," Carmen said, grumbling under her breath. "Maybe I just wanted to look nice on my birthday."

Josie, always the peacekeeper, said, "You do look nice! It's just different. But I like it!"

"I don't like it," Ganesha grumbled.

"Well, I don't like your face."

"Wow, witty. How *do* you come up with such brilliant replies?"

"I just think, what would Ganesha say, and say that."

Ganesha's eyes rolled hard. But she hadn't quite hidden her lingering smile as they piled into the car. The bad joke seemed to have settled her friend's hackles at the dress. As long as Carmen made corny jokes and Ganesha made fun of her, order was restored. Good. She should have just worn the cargo pants.

Music played in the car and gave Carmen instant nostalgia. She hadn't listened to the kind of pop-punk screaming from the speakers since high school. All vocal whine and angsty lyrics. At The Drive In! That was the name of the band playing. In fact, they would break up soon, if she wasn't mistaken. She reminded herself to look up their concert schedule to see them live before that happened. Knowing which bands would split soon wasn't exactly helpful. If only her future knowledge included lotto ticket numbers.

Arriving along the coastal highway, they found

free parking far from the pier. As they walked to their destination, she let her friends control the conversation.

"I think we should make up a club," Josie said. "I'll be president, you can be vice president, 'Nesha, and Ramen can be Club Secretary. We'll apply for funds from the school council to 'hold meetings—'" She curled her fingers into air quotes. " —but we'll really use the money for our college applications."

"It's the perfect racket!" Excitement always brought Ganesha's speaking voice several octaves higher. "It'll look good on college applications, *and* it will fund them too."

Josie's posture visibly wilted. "But what will our club be about? And I think we have to get a teacher on board as faculty oversight."

Ganesha sounded less eager now. "I think we have to have a minimum number of members to start a club. And I'm pretty sure three is too few."

The news made Josie pout. "Yeah, let's put a pin in this idea. There's potential, but it needs refining."

Weaving around a large family with strollers loaded with beach gear, Ganesha changed the subject. "I'm looking forward to AP Government with Mr. Greyland. Maybe he'll agree to be our faculty advisor?"

"He's already faculty advisor for Model UN."

Her best friends joined freshman year and stuck with it, despite complaining bitterly every year about the extra work. It was a college application MVP as far as extracurriculars went.

"Darn." Carmen pulled a face and interjected for the first time. "I guess I could join Model UN. Do they give out application fee grants?"

"I think they assume we can all pay the measly thirty

to fifty dollars," Ganesha said with ire.

Josie sighed. "Oh, the plight of living in SoCal."

Gardenville, California was known for blue ribbon schools and swanky living. The three of them were among the poor minority that scraped by in the fancy suburbs of Gardenville. Ganesha's family struggled the most with three generations crowded into a two-bedroom rental. Her dad had been a scientist in India but now worked as a taxi driver. Her mom had a master's in literature but cleaned homes for a living. Both barely spoke first-grade English between them. Carmen asked what classes her friends were taking.

"We filled the paperwork out last week." Ganesha scoffed. "You already forgot?"

"I'll email you my schedule," Josie said, using a tone meant to pacify. "I'm taking English with you and 'Nesha, AP Chem, AP Government, AP World History, Calculus, AP French, and Orchestra. I think I'll try out for the tennis team too. I suck at tennis, but our team is terrible, and I heard they'll take anyone. I need a sport on my applications."

"And who cares if the team sucks," Ganesha said, "so long as you suck less than most of them."

"Exactly."

Ganesha listed off her classes grudgingly, mostly AP classes. "I'm signing up for Model UN again. Although I cannot stand Craig. He's such a douche."

Carmen could not remember who Craig was. She didn't ask. She offered instead. "Maybe I'll join too."

"Really?" They both looked surprised at her insistence.

"I mean," Carmen said weakly, "I should probably pad my applications too."

"Yeah, I mean, I'm glad. It just doesn't seem like your

thing." Ganesha sounded apologetic since really any after-school activity wasn't Carmen's thing.

She remembered having a chip on her shoulder about the entire high school experience but didn't know why now. Crippling teen anxiety seemed like a distant memory. She resolved to change her senior year experience if she had to stick around. She still wasn't letting go of the possibility of going to bed tonight and waking up where she belonged.

At the end of the pier, they ate hot dogs and threw their leftover buns and fries at the seagulls. Eventually, they headed back toward the shoreline. An old movie theater stood close to the boardwalk. It smelled musty, the seats were perpetually sticky, and the movies were past due, but tickets were half-price — great entertainment for a couple of broke high schoolers.

The horror movie Carmen picked started in twenty minutes. They got into the concession line at Josie and Ganesha's insistence, realizing this must be part of their usual routine when she saw the guy selling snacks. She couldn't believe she'd crushed hard on this guy. He looked like a greasy, dirty child. But then, everyone looked impossibly young to her. He wore his hair in a mohawk with the ends dyed blue and black eyeliner smudged around his bright blue eyes. His prominently displayed name badge read, "Hi, I'm Mattias, happy to serve you!"

"Ramen, looking nice tonight! Special occasion?"

Clearly, her clothing choice had been poor if everyone noticed it.

"It's my birthday today, so I thought I'd dress up for the occasion."

"Happy birthday!"

"Thanks! A medium of your finest popcorn, please."

"Here, on the house tonight for your birthday." He gave her a wink and handed over the popcorn. Carmen remembered that he was friends with a lot of the theater crowd Logan spent time with.

"Hey, any parties going on before school starts?" she asked, hoping she could manufacture a meet-cute with Logan. She felt her friends' eyes drilling a hole into the back of her head for her daring. It was easy to ask, though. He was friendly, and she had no skin in this if he said no.

"Funny you should ask! I just booked a gig DJing the weekend after school starts. You should come to Jeremy's birthday party—here." He pulled a crumpled-up flier out of his wallet and handed it to her.

"Cool! Thanks! We'll be there."

A cough came from the woman behind them, a subtle reminder of the growing line.

Josie didn't let go of her arm as they moved out of sight. "You just *asked*, and he invited us to a party! Where has this energy come from? Because I am *here* for it."

"I don't know, guys." Ganesha shook her head, sounding hesitant. "Jeremy always throws these huge ragers, and the cops are called every year."

They didn't attend parties. The three of them lived on the periphery of high school social life. But a party sounded fun. And everyone talked about Jeremy's start-of-year birthday parties. She hoped Logan would be there.

The '90s horror movie was late classic to her now thought it premiered less than two months ago. She enjoyed it even though she'd seen it dozens of times and knew every jump scare. Horror movies always inversely made her happy. Something about all that campy gore and fear was cleansing.

When she got home and checked her blog, she had replies to her query about time travel. They had paid her question forward in spades, and she felt a wealth of warm feelings at their support for her.

@BearyFunny:

> "Fun! Is there a wrong that must be righted? Are they sent back to change the future? I feel like the very act of them being in the past would mean they've already changed the timeline just by existing in the past. I say they should improve the situation however they can."

@Archimedes gave her a list with source material linked. She could always count on him to come bearing an encyclopedia of knowledge.

> "1. Single continuum or predestination—characters only act to maintain the timeline. Often, in these types of stories, the characters go back in time so there are two versions of the same person from the present and future and they must avoid each other or something catastrophic might happen. These are also a closed loop, in which the time travel was always meant to happen, and what was changed was always supposed to

have been changed."

Well, there weren't two versions of her running around avoiding each other, so she could cross out this type of time travel. She'd woken up in her seventeen-year-old body. Time did not mysteriously collapse in on itself that day, even though she hadn't repeated her seventeenth birthday precisely as she had before. She couldn't repeat what she did and how she acted ten years ago. It was impossible. She wasn't that person. She had a decade of life experience between her and seventeen.

> "2. Fixed points or self-healing timelines — characters can change certain things but often the outcome is still the same. There are certain fixed points that will always happen. Time is linear and pre-determined. This isn't a perfect example but think of Macbeth. Macbeth doesn't travel through time, but is told the future. By being told what happens, he guarantees that the future happens."

This was certainly possible. Being seventeen had been a significant time in her life, although everything important had happened at the end of her senior year, like graduating, moving out, her parent's divorce, and the only other significant event she remembered, that teacher's passing. But all of that was months away! She hoped she wasn't stuck here that long.

> "3. Time loop — repetition until a

lesson is learned. This type of time travel is usually a loop that repeats again and again, like in the movie Groundhog Day."

Her seventeenth birthday from what she remembered had been entirely unremarkable ten years ago, and today. What could be so important for a seventeen-year-old girl to do? She would find out if she was in a Groundhog Day type time loop if she went to bed and woke up the morning of her seventeenth birthday again.

"4. Infinite timelines—every change creates a new timeline, so there are infinite timelines for every choice made differently. This is the type of time travel represented in Quantum Leap."

Well, she had certainly changed the day of her seventeenth birthday. With a simple outfit and asking a guy for an invite to a party, she'd changed the timeline. Did that mean she was now in a new timeline? Could she return to hers? She didn't even know how she'd gotten here in the first place. In Quantum Leap didn't they have a time machine?

Her head hurt. Maybe if she went to bed, she would wake up twenty-seven again and this would all be a fever dream.

CHAPTER

5

The following day Carmen woke disoriented to the unwelcome sight of her collage wall. Time travel. Childhood bedroom. In the past.

Well, there went that hope. Carmen rolled over and checked the date on her computer. August 24th, 1999. The day after her seventeenth birthday. At least she wasn't stuck in a Groundhog Day loop. But she was still stuck in the past.

Burrowing back into bed, she shut her eyes, not ready to face the day yet. After tossing and turning and feeling sorry for herself for several minutes, she threw herself out of bed. No more self-pity. She would get out and improve her situation.

First, she needed a driver's license. She vaguely recalled stashing her previous year's waitressing tips somewhere in her room. Those tips had gone toward her first year of community college, but she needed that money now. After tearing her room apart in her search, she found an envelope between her mattress and box spring with more than enough cash for a used car. She reacquainted herself with 1999's Craigslist and printed a couple of listings, noting several to book test drives with.

Next, she rang up Josie. Between her two best friends, the blonde was least likely to ask questions.

"Morning! How do you feel about lending me your car to get my driver's license?"

Drab cargo pants and an oversized Oasis T-shirt graced Carmen's body when Josie's hell on wheels pulled up. She got fewer comments dressed this way. She'd learned her lesson.

She passed the written test with no problems. Josie let her use her car, with reservations, to take the driving test. Carmen passed that too, of course, having ten years of driving experience. Her friend cheered when Carmen showed off her newly minted license.

"This is awesome! I thought you were scared of driving. This opens so many opportunities." It certainly did. "Will your mom let you borrow the car sometimes?"

"I'm going to look for my own," Carmen said. "I've got some money set aside."

"Good! I had no idea!"

Of course, she had no idea. That hadn't been seventeen-year-old Carmen's plan.

Celebrating with cheap drive-thru burritos, they stopped at a park Carmen and her friends frequented. The park sat roughly central to their three homes and was fashioned to resemble a pirate ship with a swing set that hung off the gangplank. Josie and Carmen rocked in adjacent swings, scarfing burritos from greasy paper bags.

Ganesha usually filled the silence with her chatter while Carmen followed along. But with her current lack of knowledge, she stayed quiet.

"Are you feeling okay?" Josie said after another pause that lengthened past comfort. This wasn't their natural state of things.

"Yeah, I'm just feeling kinda off," Carmen said vaguely. "I think I'm distracted with school starting and summer ending."

"How's your dad? I haven't seen him in a while."

Despite being an only child with the most privacy of the three of them, Carmen avoided inviting her friends over. She was honest with her friends about her situation at home. But she would rather tell than show.

"Yeah, my dad's okay. I am worried about him, though. He's going to have surgery again, I think."

"Oh man, I'm sorry. But having a car means you might be able to help him out—drive him to appointments and stuff. Hey, if you have the car in time for school to start, maybe you can give me and 'Nesha a ride. We can carpool or something."

"I'm pretty sure Ganesha would be too scared to drive with me."

Josie and Ganesha had attempted to teach her once they both earned their licenses, occasionally forcing Carmen behind the wheel in empty parking lots late at night. However, the lessons came to an abrupt halt when Carmen mixed up the gas for the brake pedal and hit a tree with Ganesha's family vehicle.

"Yeah, let's maybe give you a little more time to practice," Josie said with a grimace. She likely recalled the same memory.

Within the next couple of days Carmen picked up a

used hatchback at a steal. It was ugly as sin with peeling yellow-brown paint, cracked seats, and a dented bumper, but the engine was in decent condition. Once she was mobile, she got a bank account so she wouldn't resemble a depression-era hoarder with her money hidden under her mattress. The car came in handy for other errands too, like school shopping, changing her classes, and generally trying to improve the things she felt her life in 1999 severely lacked. She kept hoping she would wake up in her own time, but no luck.

Nervous energy filled her over her next shift at the HollyJolly. She couldn't remember her employee number, any of the menu details, or even where her uniform or badge was. On the scheduled day of her next shift, she turned her room upside down before finding both her uniform and badge crumpled at the bottom of a backpack.

The night before work, a lime green pager she forgot she owned trilled at her with a page from Jenny. She asked if Carmen needed a ride, but she declined, telling her that she was now the proud owner of her own set of wheels.

Carmen had been too shy and anxious to be more than acquaintances with the petite redhead that cursed like a sailor, had a larger-than-life personality, and a voice that could be heard across any room. They were the same age, but Jenny went to the nearby private Catholic high school. She lived in Carmen's neighborhood, thus the offer of rides.

On Saturday, Carmen showed up early to work, having to print a map to get there. Carmen's nerves were well-founded.

"Girl, are you okay today?" The redhead asked as she helped Carmen clean a spill in the kitchen. It was her second dropped plate of the night.

"Yeah, I've got a blinding headache. It's distracting." She would probably have to fake a head injury if this continued. She needed an excuse for her sudden incompetence, or she would be fired.

"Here's some Tylenol. I can run some of your food out for you. Go get some water or coffee, or something."

Carmen wouldn't have managed to finish the night without Jenny's help. She insisted she take home some of her tips.

Jenny and Carmen were the closing crew that night, which relieved Carmen. Other than Jenny, Carmen couldn't remember any of the other employees' names. And no one else had to witness Carmen fumble her way through the closing process. After counting the till and stacking chairs, they helped themselves to leftovers. There were a few perks to working in a restaurant.

"So," Jenny said around a mouthful of soup, "what classes are you signed up for?"

"I'm signed up for the basics. English and biology and US history, but I'm changing my electives. I decided to take theater, and I think I may try out for the cross-country team."

The redhead blew on her next spoonful of soup before replying.

"Really? I kind of got the impression you tried to spend as little time as possible at school."

Was no one going to let her change things without comment? Carmen stopped herself from a massive eye roll. She signed up for the cross-country team to do a little more investigating on the mom of the deaf girl—who was also the theater instructor and cross-country coach. Carmen also needed to take theater because it was

41

the only class she knew Logan took.

She missed him. She went from seeing him every day to being strangers. She didn't even have his AOL screen name. She'd checked. She would be changing that as soon as possible. Of course, she couldn't say any of this, so she went for what was becoming her generic answer.

"Yeah, but it's senior year. I've got to improve my college application if I want to go anywhere."

"Yeah? Well, I'm signed up for cross-country too, and our teams compete, so maybe we'll race together! Hey, if you ever want to train, let me know. I run nearly every day at 5 a.m., and I pass right by your condo."

"Let's do it. I'll text you." Carmen hurriedly corrected herself. "I mean, page you."

"Okay, Michael Johnson," Jenny said with a laugh. "Slow down."

"I've always seen myself as more like Usain Bolt, but I'll take Michael Johnson."

"Who?"

Darn, had he won the Olympic gold yet? Probably not.

"Nothing…he's a cartoon character you've probably never heard of."

"Oh, Anime?" the redhead said absentmindedly, tearing up some bread to dump in her soup. "Yeah, I've never seen any."

Her reputation as some sort of nerd preceded her.

The following day she jogged with Jenny. Adult and teen Carmen both were rarely found in a gym, although adult Carmen's apartment on Russian Hill was its own kind of exercise. But her seventeen-year-old body didn't have all those famous San Francisco hills to climb to the nearest tram stop, and it showed. Still, Carmen pushed through the two miles, huffing and puffing, and nearly blowing chunks by the end. She bid the redhead farewell with plans to run every other morning.

Her last day before classes started, she spent puttering around her room, preparing to face high school. She tried on nearly every item in her closet before choosing a generic band T-shirt and jeans in a fit of temper. She was sick of overthinking everything. At least if she wore something people expected, she wouldn't raise questions. She logged on to her blog and continued skimming journal entries to reacquaint herself with life at seventeen.

Several messages popped up on her screen, bringing a rush of guilt. She'd promised to provide fan art for her online friends and several of those pieces were late. Was it weird to feel intimidated by... herself? She hadn't drawn in any capacity in years. Carmen dug through her bookshelves and desk and found half-finished art scattered throughout her room. She located art supplies too and arranged them all on her desk.

Relief flooded Carmen as she found several fully done. Matching pieces with requests, she found three partially completed drawings. Two looked to be half-filled with marker, and one in colored pencil. She stared blankly at them, not sure where to start.

Carmen recalled how expensive her marker set was and how finicky they were to work with. Apprehensive, she started with the colored pencil instead. Her unease melted away as she gained confidence. Choosing and mixing colors took some effort, but there must have been some muscle memory because she instinctively pressed the pencils in such a way to achieve an even color and blend.

Luckily those only needed color added, the comic-style panels having been drawn before she made her time jump. Carmen didn't want to think about attempting one from scratch. The colors were probably flatter than she'd have done before, but it didn't look half-bad for her first effort in a decade.

Finishing the last panel, Carmen blinked dry eyes from the several hours that had passed in an art fog. She needed to get some sleep before school tomorrow. Although her room and desk were a disaster, she flipped the lights off and fell asleep before she could worry more about the coming school day.

CHAPTER 6

Carmen snoozed her alarm twice before dragging herself out of bed. Grateful she had laid out clothes and supplies for school the night before, she rushed to get ready. Leaving her art mess for after-school Carmen to deal with, she grabbed her keys and an apple on her way out the door.

She had told her mom about the car and her license a few days ago. Not trusting Carmen's sudden skill, her mom had insisted on taking a test drive with her. But after Carmen drove her through the neighborhood, on and off the highway, and parallel parked in one smooth move, her mom's reluctance melted away.

"Anak, I don't like that you did this without me. And where did the money come from? Your dad didn't give it to you, did he?"

"No, Mom, I've been saving up every penny from tips for a while."

"Okay, well, please be careful. Teenage drivers can be

so stupid. So many accidents!"

"I'll be careful."

"And you have to take care of it! I'm not paying for oil changes or new radios or whatever. We don't have the money for two cars."

"I'll use my own money, I promise."

"Okay..." her mom said, finally relenting. "I'm glad I don't have to give you rides anymore. I can take earlier shifts at work."

Carmen had forgotten how much her mom worked. She'd gotten her license, a car, a bank account, and changed her classes without anyone asking where she was going or what she was doing.

Her stomach full of butterflies, she pulled into the school parking lot early. She was going to see Logan again. But seventeen-year-old Logan, who didn't know her. She mentally went through the time travel list again.

1. ~~Single continuum~~
2. Fixed points
3. ~~Time loop~~
4. Infinite timelines

She could strike through the first and third. The first had been out of the running when she'd changed her seventeenth birthday. So far, time wasn't looping. So she was pretty sure the third option was out too. She was pretty sure she'd changed enough that the second could be crossed out, but today she would see Logan for the first time. Maybe she was here to meet him earlier? She'd make sure that happened today. Maybe then she would wake up in 2009.

When she got to her second-period theater class, he

sat at the edge of the stage with a few others. He looked like himself and yet wholly different. His hair was short, nearly buzzcut, and he wore a letterman jacket. None of the loud print, none of the carefully selected vintage pieces he treasured, and no facial hair. But his smile was the same — a dimple on the left side and those misaligned canines, expressive and sly.

When he looked up, she realized that she'd been staring. She hurriedly looked away, setting her stuff down on one of the scattered chairs.

He didn't know her. This was torture.

Trying to look busy and not stare at her future boyfriend-turned-stranger, she dug into her pocket before realizing she had no cell phone to mess with. 1999 sucked.

Mrs. Malone walked in from a back office, juggling several stacks of paper. She greeted everyone as she stumbled to the front of the room, dropping a few papers which fluttered to the ground. Mrs. Malone looked younger than her funeral photo at the reunion. The picture had shown a stilted smile and perfectly styled hair — a static faded image.

The animation in her expression made her look ten years younger. Mrs. Malone stood at the front of the room with a messy ponytail, a pencil half-dangling from an ear, as she haphazardly settled stacks of paper on the edge of her desk.

"Hello, I'm Mrs. Malone. Most of you know me as this is the senior class."

And indeed, most of the kids in the room seemed to know each other, a chorus of hellos coming from the students. Carmen was the odd one out. At least she wouldn't have to pretend to know things she didn't remember. She could start fresh with these people. Easier in some ways than talking to her family and friends.

"For those interested, the Young Thespian's Society meets on Thursdays after school, starting the second week. It is accredited with the International Thespian's Society, junior troupe number 297. It carries weight on your college applications, so consider it if you are interested. The Thespian Club is where you want to be if you want to be in the publicly held performances. We only study theater here. If you have stage fright, this is a safe space."

A few people laughed.

"Here is your syllabus." She started handing out the stacks of paper to the students. "Please review the dates of each in-class performance. I know I just said this was a safe space, and it is! Only your fellow classmates will be witnessing and critiquing your work. We will be doing character analysis and the building and creating of a dramatic character. We will do group improvisation exercises as well as monologues. I will be splitting you into groups, so don't bother finding your buddy."

Carmen's shoulders wilted as her brief hope died. She would have to leave it up to chance to do group work with Logan. Carmen looked through the syllabus and remembered why she rarely participated in extracurriculars. It was so much work. Still, some of the activities sounded fun. Like building sets, for example. Performing in front of other people? Not as much. She'd taken the class solely because Mrs. Malone taught it, and Logan took it.

"Now — why do we want art?"

Carmen's attention shifted away from the syllabus to focus on Mrs. Malone.

"What need does it satisfy?" She spoke as she paced at the front of the room. "What is the relationship between society and theater? Theater is not food, it is not water, or sunlight. Yet why do we seek it out, create it, desire it? It fulfills our desire for beauty, emotion, and connection. Art is made by those who have a burning desire to create. Art is also rebellion. Art can make the "other" relatable. Art has been used to start revolutions, point out inequality, and to bring attention to the needs of others. Now turn to page twelve and tell me what you see..."

The class ended before she knew it. She saw why Mrs. Malone's students loved her. She was a passionate teacher.

Logan left as she gathered her stuff. She hoped for some interaction, but what did she expect? They were nothing to each other.

Cross-country would be Tuesdays and Thursdays during zero period, the hour before school officially began. Thursdays would be long since she planned on joining the Young Thespian's Society — what a name — after school as well. Carmen picked up coffee for herself both mornings, which was a poor choice. Running on a stomach full of coffee was not pleasant. Still, she needed the caffeine. At least psychologically. She mentioned the coffee problem to Jenny during their next early morning run.

"They make these pre-workout drinks that are supposed to give you a ton of energy. Just take it easy on them. They're a lot of kick if you're not careful."

At a workout supplement shop she picked some up. She took less than half the dose the package recommended, but it helped pick her up in the morning before running. She took a full dose the next time and felt as if her heart would beat out of her chest. Did they sell this stuff to just anyone? It didn't seem safe. She reminded herself to ask Mrs. Malone if she drank pre-workout and warn her off it. She didn't know if the innocuous powdered drink could trigger a stroke, but it seemed prudent to exclude it as a cause.

The after-school Young Thespian's Society was held on the second Thursday of the school year. The meeting was in the theater again, with the chairs all neatly stacked at the back of the room and the stage's red curtains lit up. Students took some of the folding chairs and put them in a semi-circle near the front of the open room. Grabbing a chair and pulling it into a gap between students, she listened in on several conversations.

"I hear she wants us to do fewer musicals this year," said a guy with close-cropped hair, "which is disappointing, but I guess I get it. Society did *only* musicals all of last year."

Carmen guessed 'Society' was student slang for the club's long obnoxious name. She'd felt silly calling it "The Young Thespian's Society," even in her own head. She'd worked out the acronym but calling it TYTS wasn't any better.

Logan, who sat across from Carmen, spoke up at this. "I hope we do at least one musical. I was planning to send one of the recordings from this year to the music program I'm applying to."

"You can always use material from last year," someone piped up.

A girl sitting closer to Carmen split from the

conversation with the girl next to her, making it difficult for Carmen to listen in.

"I'm glad," the girl said, smoothing the skirt of her cheerleading uniform. "Last year, I was relegated to poodle-skirt girl number two because I can't hold a tune."

Another person's voice overlapped. "Since Juan graduated last year, I'd like to be stage manager."

Logan turned to someone else in the group and began a private conversation, which Carmen strained to hear. She heard the words *party* and *Jeremy* and guessed at their topic of discussion. This was the same party that movie theater mohawk guy, Mattias, invited her to. Logan looked enthusiastic, like he had plans to attend. She was going to that party, and she would drag her friends there somehow.

"Hello, young thespians!" Mrs. Malone waltzed in from the same back office, sans paper stacks. "I see many familiar faces but a couple of new ones, so I'll just make brief announcements." She repeated the same spiel she'd given in theater class, but Carmen was grateful for the reminder.

Carmen's applications severely lacked extracurriculars. Her grades weren't good enough to make an impression either. The first time she'd lived through senior year, her previous lackluster college submissions led to a mailbox full of rejection letters. If she was truly stuck in 1999, her application would be more promising this time around.

Mrs. Malone confirmed they would not be doing musicals this year. Rather, they would be doing book or movie-to-play adaptations, which spurred groans from some and cheers from others. She explained that they would choose three and that the first would premiere the week after Thanksgiving, the second the week before

Easter, and the third the week before spring finals.

All the plays performed her senior year Carmen remembered. She'd gone to see them because she liked theater, and this club put together decent productions.

Logan suggested *Peter Pan*, and she knew that would be one of them. Another suggested *Alice in Wonderland*, and another the *Wizard of Oz*. She knew those would be selected too. Several others were presented, including *Frankenstein*, *Cinderella*, and *Charlie and the Chocolate Factory*. Carmen did not offer any but voted for the three she knew would win.

After the plays were chosen by consensus, Mrs. Malone instructed the students to split into groups based on what they wanted to contribute to the play — acting or backstage crew. Having no experience acting, Carmen joined the stage crew to learn what this required. The more experienced people in the group were quickly elected by consensus to manage lighting and sound, set and prop building, and costume making. Carmen eavesdropped on Logan as much as she could but found her interest in the backstage work drawing her back.

Volunteering, Carmen joined the set builders. Adult Carmen did no arts or crafts, but in the last few weeks, she'd drawn more than she had in the last ten years. She found herself looking forward to the projects ahead.

The hour passed quickly, and before she knew it, everyone was getting ready to leave. She tried to think of some reason to start a conversation with Logan, but he again left before she had the chance.

Mrs. Malone noticed her loitering and walked over.

"Hello, Ms. Santos?"

"Hi, Mrs. Malone."

"I see you're in many of my classes this semester. I

52

don't believe you've done theater or cross-country in previous years, so just ask if you need any extra help."

What could Carmen say to continue the conversation? "I've joined the prop building group. Do you have any suggestions for working on my acting for the next play?"

"Try out. If you want some practice without an audience, though, we will do a lot of acting in class, so you'll get more training then."

"I'd like to be able to tryout by the time we get to *Wizard of Oz*. It's one of my favorite books."

"Me too. I was glad someone suggested it. Try a small role in the next play to get comfortable on stage, and by the time we get to *Wizard of Oz* in the spring, you'll be ready for a bigger role."

"Thank you. I'll do that."

It wasn't a smooth segue, but she worked it in any way. "I wanted to know, for cross-country, I'm really dragging in the mornings, so I've been drinking coffee, but it makes me kinda nauseous. I want to try some pre-workout..." She hesitated, and Mrs. Malone jumped in enthusiastically.

"I live off a mix of protein and pre-workout in the mornings. I can show you a few brands I like. I save the coffee for after running."

"Thanks, but isn't that pre-workout stuff terrible for you?" Carmen said, "Like couldn't it cause a stroke or a heart attack?"

"Everyone's a doctor." Mrs. Malone shook her head like she'd heard criticism on this subject before. "I promise you, it's fine. I've been drinking energy drinks, pre-workout, and coffee for years, and I'm healthy. You're young. You'll be okay."

High amounts of stimulants weren't great for the

circulatory system. Still, it took more than average stimulants to have a stroke in your late 40s, as Mrs. Malone was going to.

But there was no good way for a seventeen-year-old to lecture her teacher on her health, so she thanked her for the advice and left for home.

The school week had been a moderate success. She made contact with Mrs. Malone, but Logan was still a stranger to her. She hoped he would attend the party that weekend.

CHAPTER 7

School raced into Friday, and Carmen was scheduled to work the dinner shift. When she walked into the HollyJolly that night, Jenny was there again. The redhead had been a lifesaver the previous shift. The girl had only ever been an acquaintance before, but Carmen resolved to be a better friend to her. With that in mind, between orders, she asked Jenny if she wanted to go to the party the next day.

"Girl, yes! I was already going, but I'm glad you are." She held her hands and squealed.

Surprised at her fervor, Carmen gave her a puzzled look. "It's just a party."

"You never come to this stuff. I've invited *you* before, but you never come."

"Yeah, well..." Carmen tapered off, not having anything to say to that. Had Jenny invited her before? Carmen couldn't remember.

"I stopped asking you when you never said yes. A bunch of us are going, actually." Jenny gestured to the busy waitstaff bustling around them.

"Want to carpool?"

"I'm driving with my friends, but let's meet there."

She had convinced Josie to go too, but Ganesha was still on the fence. Ganesha didn't want to get in trouble with her parents. Her family was very traditional, so she would have to lie to go. In fact, they all would have to lie to go. Although their parents would likely never suspect it of them, they'd never gone to a party in their lives at this age. They hadn't so much as ditched a class or sipped alcohol until college. They were good kids. Too good. In Carmen's opinion, all three of them needed to loosen up a bit.

On Saturday morning, Carmen ran with Jenny again. After finishing her usual chores, she found several messages from her online friends inquiring about the last week. She'd been so absorbed in getting back to school and reacclimating to teenage life, her posting frequency was non-existent. Her online friends must have felt ghosted because the messages had piled up, especially from those waiting on art she'd promised.

Replying to several people, she then scanned the finished colored pencil piece to send. After that was done, she felt the weight of the half-finished marker pieces mocking her from their corner shelf. They'd haunted her subconscious the last few weeks, knowing they were past due.

Instead, Carmen practiced with scrap paper—a quick sketch of her bed and bookshelf, then marker to color it in. Her past self continued to impress. She couldn't figure out how to balance the colors and the piece turned out blotchy and muddy. Disgusted, she set her art away to type a journal entry.

"Hello Internet! School and work have been a little nuts. I had a change of heart about a bunch of my classes and electives last minute and may have bitten off more than I can chew. I'm sorry if you're waiting on a commission, I promise I'm working on them! School has just swallowed up all my time. If I fail everything, my mom may just do what she's always threatened and kick me out! No daughter of hers will be a failure!

Speaking of being dramatic, I've decided to take drama! And join cross-country. I've just been thinking about my future and what I want it to be like. And I can't put fan-artist down as extracurriculars on my college application. But all this work and stress can wait for tomorrow me to worry about as I'm off to a party tonight! To hopefully flirt with a boy I like. Wish me luck!"

She would get back to 2009 somehow, and getting to know Logan's younger self would help her figure out her feelings for him. She loved him, but was she ready for marriage? Was he right for her? For forever? Could she *do* forever?

She'd been teenage-Carmen for a few weeks now, and she still wasn't any closer to figuring out how to get back to 2009, except to live one day at a time. So, she might as well make her time in high school fun. When she was a senior before, she'd taken everything so seriously. Why couldn't she just go to a party and have some fun?

She told her dad where she was going, and he'd given her a simple "be careful," distracted by the evening news. Josie gave him a wave from the doorway as she closed the door behind her. The night rolled in warm and smelling of summer. The asphalt was still hot as she walked to her friend's hell on wheels. Ganesha sat shotgun as always, so she climbed into the cracked backseat.

"What are you wearing?" Ganesha turned around to look at Carmen as she secured her seatbelt.

"Nothing. Absolutely no clothing at all. I don't know why you sound so surprised."

"I've never seen you wear a dress until your birthday and now you're wearing a dress again."

In the last few weeks, she'd bought some clothes and asked to take more shifts at the HollyJolly to make up for the added expense. She planned on slowly rotating in the dresses and other assorted items she liked for a smoother transition. But clearly, Ganesha noticed and did not like it.

"I can't always wear cargo pants," Carmen muttered resentfully.

Changing the subject, Josie piped up, sounding nervous. "You sure they'll just let us in? I don't even know Jeremy."

"Or we could just go get some tacos and hang out at Pirate Park like we usually do," Ganesha said.

Tapping the steering wheel, Josie looked around to exit the parking lot. "Should we have brought something? Like, a present? Or is this a potluck?"

Carmen deserved a medal for holding back an almighty eye roll. Had the three of them always been this... socially anxious? Carmen ignored Ganesha's comment. They were going if she had to drag them.

"It's a party. Jeremy won't know half the people there. Everyone at work was talking about it, and half of them don't even go to Jamboree. It's fine. Jenny is coming, and she said she's bringing alcohol. I can drive us home if you guys want to drink?"

Twisting at the waist, Ganesha talked over the center console. "I am definitely not drinking. I barely wanted to come to this thing, but you guys need a DD. I'll drive us home. Plus, you barely have your license, Ramen. I'm gonna need to see proof of a clean driving record for at least six months before I'll trust you to drive me."

Carmen did roll her eyes then.

Just as they exited the condo complex, Josie called toward the backseat, where Carmen dug through her purse for Chapstick. "So, where are we going?"

"Google it?" Carmen said absentmindedly.

"What?"

"Oh shoot, yeah." Carmen had an address and a flier but hadn't thought to get directions beforehand. 1999 didn't have cell phones to tell them where to go.

"I'm sorry," Carmen sheepishly said. "We're going to have to go back. I forgot to print directions."

Ganesha's irritated expression came with a long-suffering sigh for Carmen. Josie turned them around and Carmen jumped out and ran back to her room. She made quick work of MapQuest before jogging back to the car with a printout.

"Don't worry. It's not crazy far. It's in the fancy custom homes right by the high school."

And indeed, when they pulled onto the right street, they passed houses with huge, manicured lawns that were neatly divided by tall hedges. They pulled up to a house that sat against a canyon wall and had that boxy glass modern look only expensive custom homes seemed to have. Other teenagers meandered up a stone path between manicured landscapes of flowers, grass, and rock, and walked through wide open doors. Loud music reverberated off the canyon wall, and wavering light from the pool shimmered behind the house.

When she walked in, Jenny and a few of her friends from Catholic school and work lounged in a fancy velvet chaise just inside the entryway. Carmen and Jenny made introductions all around. They already seemed a bit tipsy and handed her and Josie a bottle of cheap twist-off wine to share. Ganesha crinkled her nose and declined. Josie's mouth pursed at her first sip, but she took another.

They wove through the crowd before spilling out into the backyard where the music was loudest. Mattias stood under a gazebo with giant speakers and a sort of DJ contraption of lights, vinyl, and wires standing before him. Carmen covertly looked for Logan as they walked through the house but didn't see him until they stepped outside. He wore his pants rolled up, legs dangling over the edge into the massive pool. Jeremy and a crowd of other guys, presumably from the water polo team too, sat next to him.

Having no interest in getting wet, the girls found open seating around an unlit bonfire pit. Summer still warmed the air around them, with no need for jackets or fires.

Their conversation meandered from past summers to college plans. Carmen covertly watched Logan, and when he got up alone to go inside, she made her excuses and walked in after him. Logan headed toward the kitchen and the keg set up. She queued up behind him, and as they waited, their eyes caught and held.

"Hey, you joined the Society, right?" he said to her with an inquisitive smile. Oh. She missed that smile, even this half-polite thing, a shadow of his full sly grin.

"The what?" Carmen said.

"You know, the Thespian's Society club? We call it the Society because saying 'Thespian' makes us all sound like nerds."

"Yeah!" she said. *Too enthusiastic,* she thought. *Cool it, Carmen.*

"I'm Logan." He held his hand out to her, and she shook it, feeling that this moment was important.

How does one shake the hand of a future boyfriend? Firmly? Add a fist bump? Try not to hold on too long or let go too fast? After catching his hand in a shake, she realized that he meant it as more of a friendly wave, her forced handshake odd and formal. She let go quickly, and he chuckled. Not a mean-spirited laugh, just a surprised huff. His smile went from polite to crooked, a tease to the angle of his grin and the dimple fully formed. Real.

"Hi, I'm Carmen. Yeah, I joined the Society. And your theater class too."

"Oh yeah? Cool, I love Mrs. Malone. I've been in the Society since freshman year."

"That's cool! I've seen all your plays. I mean, *the—*" she emphasized "*—plays.* You, ah, you guys are really good."

"Thanks! I really appreciate it." His voice was enthusiastic and genuine. He didn't notice or purposefully didn't call attention to her awkwardness, other than the slight curl of his lip at her handshake.

"You should be proud. All of you." She rambled, not sure what to say but wanting to continue talking. "I

really liked Grease last year. You've got a great voice."
Someone stop her from talking. She was being way too
obvious. "I mean, you played Danny, right? Or was that
someone else?"

"No, I played Danny. And thanks, it means a lot
when you put so much work into something, and people
appreciate it." He quirked his lips up.

"I'm looking forward to the plays we're doing this
year."

"Me too," he said, sounding enthused before continuing in a somewhat less ebullient tone. "Though I
was really hoping for more music because it's my senior
year. I'm applying to some programs that need music
submissions."

At the front of the short line, he poured her a beer
first, then poured himself one. She held her plastic cup
up to clink together and said, "*Proste!*"

"Cheers," he said. "What does *proste* mean?"

"It's German for cheers." She held her glass out again.
"Or we could say *Egészségére.*" She pronounced it with the
SH sound for SZ, which was the correct way of saying it.
"It's Hungarian for cheers. Well, actually, it's Hungarian
for 'To Your Health and Good Digestion,' but the idea is
generally the same."

His attempt to repeat the word only butchered it.
They both sniggered over his effort. She tutted at him,
pulling her glass away when he tried to tap his to hers.

"Nope," she said. "Hungarians don't clink glasses."

Following each other out, they talked as they meandered through the party, before reaching the open back
door. They stopped and leaned on opposite door jambs,
breathing in the fresh air.

"Why do they have a word for cheers if they aren't

actually going to do the thing?"

"The story goes that when Hungary was invaded by, I think, the Austrians? After defeating them in battle, the Austrian soldiers clinked glasses over their dead bodies. Now Hungarians never clink glasses."

"Gruesome!" The surprise delighted tone in his voice must have meant he approved. "And how do you know so much about Hungary? Are you Hungarian? Is that what you call a person from Hungary? I know nothing about Hungary except how to toast." He smiled mischievously at her.

Flutter like bubbles popped in her chest at the conspiratorial look. The answering expression she gave him was shy.

"No, I'm Filipino. I just like collecting random facts." She shrugged. She couldn't say she'd been there. It wouldn't check out because seventeen-year-old Carmen had never been out of the United States. Fishing around for some way to continue the conversation, she said, "Did you know that *Salud* is how you say cheers in Spain?"

"I did know that one."

"Hmm." She thought of other interesting cheers she could recall. "How about *skoal*?" She held her glass out, and he asked if it was safe to clink with this toast. She clinked his glass as permission.

"Yes, that's Swedish for cheers. Actually, it's cheers for most of the Nordic countries."

"The Vikings did love their alcohol," Logan mused. "You aren't just a collector of random facts. You've specifically collected a lot of trivia on alcohol."

"I know, it's weird." She felt her cheeks flush.

"No, it's interesting! Got anymore? I'm trying to start a band, and you're giving me great ideas for band names."

"Well, I'm Filipino, so '*Mabuhay. La votre*' is French. Which means 'yours,' but people also say 'A *ta sante!*'" She held her glass out again, and he clinked it with a flourish, his pinky out.

"I Like '*la votre*'," he said. "If I convince my buddies to play, we'll invite you to our first show."

"I'll try not to be too harsh a critic, but I make no promises." She sniffed, holding her nose up high.

"Ouch!" He clutched at his chest, playing wounded.

She rolled her eyes at him, a half-smile slipping past her nonchalant façade.

A large splash from the pool grabbed their attention. The birthday boy now stood in the pool laughing, fully dressed, and soaking wet. He took his sopping shirt off and threw it at his friends who were trying to help him out of the water.

"Looks like Jeremy has overdone it already." Logan gestured to them. "I'm gonna help the other guys get him out of the pool or join him so he doesn't drown. It was fun talking with you, Carmen. *Mabuhay*." He smiled that knee-weakening foxy grin and held his glass out again to clink as they parted ways. He even got the emphasis correct on the last syllable. Impressive.

When she realized her friends across the yard watched with interest, she wiped the sloppy look off her face.

"Who was that handsome boy," Jenny stage whispered as Carmen approached.

"That was Logan." Ganesha answered for her, matter of factly. "He goes to our school."

Carmen blushed. "He's just in a couple of my classes, is all. He is cute, though, isn't he?"

"Yes! If all public-school boys looked like him, I'd change schools," the redhead said with a lascivious look in his direction. He was in the pool, his shirt thrown off, trying to help his friend out of the pool. The view was... ideal.

"Hey! Dibs!" Carmen gave her a shove, both for the tease and to make room on the yard furniture she sat on.

"You can't call dibs on someone. That's...whatever the female version of misogynistic is." Josie wrinkled her nose at them, but a smile tugged at the corner of her mouth.

"She means we're objectifying him." Jenny nudged Carmen. "*Buutt*...I'm sure he's got a brilliant mind behind that pretty face." The redhead made a pinching motion with her hand as if she were squeezing an invisible bottom.

Another of her friends chimed in, catching on. "He's probably got the whole *big* package." The girl held her hands out as if measuring something. They dissolved into giggles.

Once the conversation moved on, Ganesha leaned over. "I'm surprised. He doesn't seem like your type."

Yeah, certainly not her type in high school. Although, did types matter? At seventeen, she hadn't known what she wanted. Adult Carmen wasn't sure what she wanted either if her reaction to Logan's proposal was anything to go by. All she did know was that she missed him and seeing him today was a bright spot in a long, anxiety-filled week.

Once the next song ended, Mattias put on a popular radio station and stepped inside the house for a few minutes before reappearing next to Carmen's group with a beer in hand.

"Hello, my favorite movie-buffs! Glad you guys could make it for my set."

None of them knew anything about the electronic music he played, but they all gave generic positive feedback.

"Thanks, I know Jeremy's older brother. He owns the club in Los Angeles I'd like to DJ at when I'm old enough. For now, high school parties and school dances are in my near future."

Carmen introduced Mattias to Jenny and the friends she'd come with, making room for him to sit. Josie went off to find the bathrooms and returned with a male student who looked vaguely familiar to Carmen. He was tall, with slicked-back hair and thick glasses. He didn't introduce himself, just stood awkwardly by Josie. After a few minutes, he interrupted the flow of conversation, looking down at his plastic solo cup with a wrinkle on his nose.

"You know, Jeremy really should have sprung for better beer. This stuff is absolute swill." He set his cup on their table and pushed it away, clearly done with it.

Jenny offered him some of the cheap wine, which he also declined with a sniff. He then pulled a flask out of his pocket and took a swig from it instead. He didn't offer any, but continued to loom nearby, aloof, looking out at the gathered revelers for a while, before turning to Josie and Ganesha.

"So, you'll be joining Model UN again?"

Vague affirmations was all either would give.

"There's a scholarship you may qualify for if you run for an office position. I know how much it's been a struggle to find funds for college." He said this part with a condescending pat on Ganesha's shoulder. "Obviously, president is taken." He gestured to himself. "But the treasurer position is open. If I can trust you with the club's money." He laughed as if this wasn't incredibly offensive. Maybe in another tone, it would have sounded like a joke. From him, it sounded like the insult it was.

Before either could think of an appropriate response, he made some excuse about spotting some other sycophant he knew and walked away.

"Wow. Is he always like that?" Jenny looked vaguely horrified.

Josie and Ganesha both rolled their eyes in nearly identical expressions of annoyance.

"That's him when he's trying to be nice," Josie said. "But we have to put up with him since he's president and a lot of the other officers are his cronies. Model UN is basically the star of my college application."

"Oh yeah, Craig. The overbearing president of Model UN Josie and Ganesha grumbled about." Carmen wasn't a member, so she only knew him from her friends' many complaints. Josie pointed out that he lived in the house next door. It looked like a castle and even had a turret with vines growing up the side. Carmen thought it looked obnoxious and pretentious, but that was probably because of the person who lived there.

Close to midnight, the party began winding down. No one called the cops on the underage party, despite the noise and commotion. Ganesha grew remote and awkward as the party went on and relaxed when the group started gathering their purses to leave. They had to pull Josie away, who was starting to slur her words. Maybe Carmen should have kept a closer eye on the blonde's alcohol intake. Carmen felt pleasantly tipsy, having learned her limits in college after a few too many hungover mornings and nights over the toilet.

Ganesha offered to give Jenny and her friends a ride,

but the redhead said her older brother promised to pick them up soon. Mattias had equipment to pack up and only had the one drink earlier, it mainly being a night of work for him. So, Carmen was confident he'd make it home safely.

Carmen spotted Logan again as the other girls took turns at the restroom. She knew it was strange for a girl he barely knew to check in, but no one was driving drunk on her watch.

"Hey! You have a ride, right?"

"That's really cool of you." He put a hand on her arm, and she felt his warmth through the layer of cloth like a brand. "I'm staying here tonight to help clean up in the morning." Logan gestured at the abandoned red solo cups strewn about and Logan's friends doing keg stands, spilling foamy beer in the process.

"You're a better friend than I would be." She wrinkled her nose at the mess.

He just shrugged with a smile.

Maybe she stood a moment too long, that grin doing funny things to her insides. Ganesha saved her from continued gawking and pulled her away to help shove the resistant blonde into the car.

CHAPTER 8

The next couple of weeks passed in a blur of running, drawing, studying, and working more hours at the HollyJolly. Carmen and Logan exchanged pleasantries in class and in the hallways, but their conversations never progressed beyond a few exchanged words. They were in the Society and theater class together but held different roles in the play *Alice in Wonderland*. While Logan was cast as the Cheshire Cat, she and the other stage builders moved past planning to construction.

It was hard to keep up with her online community of writers and artists since she was out of practice. She drew a few more practice pieces before she risked starting one of the commissioned marker comics. Knowing their deadlines were past due, she finished both in an overnight frenzy, hopped up on sour candy and tea.

Her friend @Archimedes asked her how her time-traveling comic was going. Carmen couldn't admit that she'd used her online community's hive mind to help with her predicament without sounding crazy. So instead, she continued the charade.

> "I'm plotting it out still, so there's nothing to show yet, and I haven't decided how it ends, but so far, our hero is trying to change the journey for the better."

She didn't know why she was in the past and couldn't tell if her attempts to improve things were working. Ganesha seemed bothered by the changes and had commented about all the time Carmen spent with Jenny, who until that summer was just a work friend.

Carmen and Jenny ran in the mornings, and they had all gone to another high school party. This time to the house of a girl from Jenny's school. Logan hadn't been there, but most of the kids who attended were from the Catholic school.

Their night ended when Josie threw up in the bathroom, and they sobered her up at the Pirate Park until the wee hours of the morning—it being the only place she could recover without witnesses. Ganesha's parents caught her as she snuck back in at nearly 3 a.m. and ended up grounded for two weeks. Carmen talked about it with Josie the next day after school while they ate burritos at Pirate Park.

"I can understand why she's kind of frustrated," Josie said when Carmen complained about Ganesha's recent bad mood. "She's the only one who got in trouble, and she wasn't the one throwing up in a bush. I was the one who got drunk. I promise, I'll cool it next time."

"Yeah, but she didn't even have any fun! It's

annoying!" Carmen dug her toe into the sand as they sat side by side on the swings.

"Why does her having or not having fun annoy you?"

"Well…" Carmen said defensively. "I don't know, I guess because we had fun?"

"Yeah, but you can't control her ability to have fun or not. Do you like playing video games?"

"No…" The non sequitur perplexed Carmen.

"Well, she does. She never forces you to play, does she?"

Josie knew this for a fact. They played when she wasn't around. Carmen was all thumbs and no skill.

"No…"

"Then let's do something together we'll all enjoy next time."

Ganesha's favorite thin-crust pizza was ordered, with white sauce and garlic. Josie and Carmen had it delivered during school lunch to make it up to her.

"Is it my birthday?" she said suspiciously when they set it on the table in front of her.

"It's an apology pizza for getting grounded." Carmen lifted a hot greasy slice, cheese stretching out obscenely. "I promise we'll have a low-key Halloween once you're free, just the three of us."

That Halloween, Carmen's parents made a bake-at-home lasagna for the three of them. They dressed up in Halloween pajamas and ate enough candy for twenty people. Her parents let them use the TV until late into the night so they could watch a marathon of horror movies. They handed candy out to the neighborhood kids and exclaimed over all the costumes. A lot of Matrix characters in long black trench coats and sunglasses showed up along with a few Spice Girls and a bunch of kids in Scream ghost masks.

Once her parents went to sleep, Carmen cajoled the other two into her car to participate in some good-ol' fashioned teenage high jinks. They brought toilet paper and eggs to TP a house but chickened out at the last minute. Instead, they bought soft-serve ice cream at a nearby drive-through and returned to Carmen's house to continue their movie marathon. Then, as 2 a.m. drew near, they fell asleep in a pile of sleeping bags and pillows on the living room floor.

Carmen woke to her parents' whisper-fighting in the kitchen. They talked in partial Tagalog and English, a combination her parents often spoke with each other.

"You knew I had to work this morning, and I asked you to pack me a lunch. Nothing is made," her mom said, her loud whisper making the words sound like a hiss.

"You can just take leftover lasagna."

"There isn't enough left, and I'll be working a double today because we're a month behind on the electricity. They'll shut it down soon if I don't send them a check."

"My disability money will be coming in a few days."

"Yes—and? It's almost nothing. Or did you forget how bills work?" her mom said. "End of the month means more bills, and the home insurance will be due soon too!"

"I don't know what to tell you." Carmen could imagine the shrug from his even voice.

"Just pack my lunch when I ask!" Her mom's voice broke above a whisper.

Josie snorted in her sleep and rolled over. Her parents went quiet.

"Okay, here, I think there's a frozen burrito at the back of the freezer—*hay nako!*"

She could see her dad's silhouette as he attempted to bend down to the bottom freezer drawer, then twisted up in pain.

"You're useless," her mom said under her breath. "Go sit down. I have to do everything myself."

Her dad sat at the kitchen table and glanced at their pile of blankets. Carmen quickly shut her eyes, feigning sleep. She hoped the other two girls would do the same if the ruckus woke them. Her mom could be heard slamming cupboards before leaving the house without a goodbye. Her dad got up and slowly shuffled back into the master bedroom. Carmen sat up and looked at the clock. 5:38 a.m. Her friends didn't stir. Carmen hoped they hadn't witnessed her parents' fight.

At least her mom hadn't started throwing or breaking anything. Carmen had been so busy lately that she hadn't kept track of the mood in the house. She would try to be more aware and help her dad out. She hated the stress, pressure, and anxiety that boiled under the surface of her parents' interactions during the first time she'd been seventeen. And she hadn't had a car to escape in then!

In the general rush and excitement of somehow being in the past, going to high school, and getting to know Logan and Mrs. Malone, she'd forgotten about her family's imminent implosion. She wasn't even sure when her dad would have his next surgery. She knew it was around the holidays. Around the same time her grandmother on her mom's side of the family would fly in from the Philippines to help out.

She'd only met her grandmother a handful of times and only knew that part of the family as the heavily accented people on the phone. If forced, she could probably recall their names from memory, but otherwise, her knowledge of her extended family was scant.

Her mom always called her siblings at weird hours of the night, talking in staccato-fast Tagalog. Every Autumn, like clockwork, her mom would collect all of their used belongings and ship them to the Philippines in large cardboard boxes called balikbayan boxes. She constantly scoured Goodwill and Salvation Army stores for items to mail to her family. Growing up, Carmen often complained of favorite toys or clothes suddenly going missing, only to find her belongings at the bottom of a Balikbayan box about to be shipped across the world.

When Carmen objected, her mom scolded her. "*Walang hiya ka!*" which roughly translated to, "You have no shame!" Her mom often called her "*hiya*" for short when she judged her to be greedy, ungrateful, or shameless.

"Your cousins have nothing, and you deny them this! You have too many toys. America spoils you!" This was often accompanied by a threat to send her to the Philippines to "teach her respect."

Her dad's parents had died when he was young. Consequently, he was raised by his grandparents and didn't have much family. Just a sister in Hawaii who called every birthday and holiday and sent cards. Her mom often complained about it to Carmen when she was mad at him.

"I should have known he wouldn't care about family. He has none!"

While her mom turned nasty during fights, her dad turned meek. It was frustrating. She was pretty sure his meekness just made her mom angrier.

Carmen couldn't fall back to sleep. She tossed and turned until Josie stirred, her blonde hair a tangled mess.

Carmen gave up trying to get more rest and instead puttered around the kitchen, making a cup of coffee and some toast to nibble on. Josie got up to use the restroom after her alarm went off before Ganesha finally stirred, groggy and irritable. None of them discussed her fighting parents. It was barely a rumble on the Richter scale of fights between them. Even so, Josie kept giving her looks as if she had heard her parents' fight while Ganesha remained oblivious.

Carmen missed her adult life. She missed her autonomy. She did not want to relive the ticking time bomb of her parents' marriage, knowing what would come and not knowing how to stop it.

It was, unfortunately, a school day. Carmen drove alone while Josie and Ganesha carpooled. Carmen was glad for the reprieve from her friends' company, despite having so much fun the night before. The tense morning was awkward enough without Josie's concerned glances.

With the play *Alice in Wonderland* a few weeks away, Carmen's set crew scheduled Wednesday evenings for painting and building. The actors used the theater on different nights, so she only saw Logan in passing. Despite Logan being the entire reason, she signed up for Society, Carmen found the manual labor of building props satisfying and the engineering behind them fascinating. The prop team figured out a way to make the Cheshire Cat magically appear and disappear during his closing number. It took some creative lighting and stage magic to make it work, but it looked amazing from the audience.

In theater class, the syllabus showed another group project coming up. They'd already done one, and Carmen was not in Logan's group. However, she figured out that Mrs. Malone had just counted out the students' seats to make each group. Carmen made sure to sit exactly seven chairs away from Logan to be placed with him during Thursday's class. She squirmed at how her meticulous planning felt like stalking, but what else was she to do? She needed to get closer to Logan somehow.

After Mrs. Malone sorted everyone into their groups — with Carmen and Logan in the same group as planned — she told them about their projects. "I want you to pick a scene from your favorite play. Five minutes tops. For the Thespian Club students, you can pick a play we will be working on this year. Pick a dramatic scene and change it somehow. Make it funny, make it sad, make it contemporary. I want a remix. This will be part of your final."

Everyone groaned.

"Come on, this is fun!" Mrs. Malone tutted. "I could just quiz you on all the Shakespearian plays we've covered so far. Would you rather do that?"

Louder groaning came from the class.

"Good. We'll reconvene in twenty minutes and finish out with an explanation of why stage lighting is so vital to good theater."

Carmen, Logan, and a girl in a cheerleading uniform sat in a tight knot of chairs at the back of the room. Logan gave Carmen his full thousand-watt grin and held up his water bottle to toast. He butchered the German word for cheers, "Prost!" But his memory had her blushing. He remembered.

Carmen introduced herself to the cheerleader, and the cheerleader introduced herself as Kelly. Carmen recognized her with shock. Of all people, the cheerleader was the girl Ganesha had been flirting with ten years in the future at their reunion. Until now, Carmen took little notice of her fellow classmates, her focus on Logan and Mrs. Malone being all-consuming.

"Hey, so I'm kind of at a loss for this one," Kelly said. She pulled a notebook from her pristine white Jansport.

"Maybe we could somehow make Macbeth or Hamlet funny?" Logan said.

Thinking of her favorite play *Wicked*, Carmen started to speak before hesitating. "I have some suggestions…" Was this plagiarism? She wasn't planning on selling her future memories of *Wicked* as her own work.

"We're all ears." Logan tapped a pen to his ear.

Carmen plowed on, pushing her uncertainty aside. "How about we do a scene from the bad guy's perspective, like show the Wicked Witch in a sympathetic light? Maybe she's just misunderstood. Or—" She was getting too close to the plot of the soon-to-be hit Broadway musical. "—show Hook in a sympathetic light somehow."

"Ooooh, I like that idea!" Kelly enthusiastically jotted down some notes.

Looking thoughtful, Logan tapped his pen against the table. "You know, I read somewhere that Hook wasn't even a part of the story when *Peter Pan* was being written. Peter Pan was supposed to be the villain."

"He is mischievous, which is like, bad guy adjacent. He and Tinkerbell aren't actually very nice," Kelly said, curling a lock of her brown hair around her finger.

"Yeah!" Carmen, excited now, talked rapidly as she made notes too. "I mean, if you look at the story differently, Peter Pan is taking children away in the middle of the night, antagonizing Hook, and always playing pranks that could seriously hurt others. And Tinkerbell actually tries to kill Wendy."

"Oooh," Kelly said, "what if we made it like a horror, and Peter Pan and Tinkerbell *feed* Hook to the Crocodile." Impressive. Sweet, preppy cheerleader Kelly had a dark side. Carmen, who loved a good horror movie, was all in.

When Mrs. Malone called time, they rushed to exchange house numbers. They decided on a meeting time and place for the next weekend at Logan's. Carmen gleefully wrote down his address. Finally! More time with Logan.

CHAPTER 9

Her dad's back surgery approached fast, scheduled for the first weekend of winter break. Carmen volunteered to take him to the surgery consultation so her mom wouldn't have to take time off. Carmen, having been a nurse in a hospital and knowing the injuries that could happen with a bad fall, made her dad take the walker, even though he was embarrassed to use it.

After vitals, questionnaires, and a long wait in the lobby, the doctor finally called them in.

"Mr. Santos, I looked at your X-rays, and it looks like we'll need to do a spinal fusion, so we'll schedule your lab work for a week before and some physical therapy before and after. Now, if you don't have any questions..."

Her dad shook his head.

"Thank you, if you'll just..." The doctor stood to usher them out.

He was not going to rush them out with so little information. Carmen didn't stand up and held her hand out to stop her dad from moving.

"Excuse me, doctor, but a spinal fusion of what? He's had a spinal fusion of the lower back." She turned to her dad. "But you still have pain in your neck and lower back, right?" At her dad's nod, Carmen turned back to the doctor. "So, he needs work in the cervical and lumbar region?"

The doctor sat back down, giving her a measured look. "Well, you've done your research, young lady, yes."

Carmen indicated that she'd like to see the X-ray, so he put it on the light screen. She was no X-ray tech, but she'd seen a fair few X-rays and could see his previous hardware in his lower back glowing. It looked like some of the hardware had moved. She also noted the overgrown bone glowing on the X-ray. The bone, as a defense mechanism against his serious injury and the added foreign hardware, had built more bone. The X-ray of her dad's lower back and neck region looked like Christmas had come early.

"Which vertebrae are affected?" she asked.

The doctor's eyebrows went up in surprise. "Well, it sounds like you understand some anatomy. I'll give you the medical terminology and ask me if you don't understand a term I use." He turned to the X-ray. "His injury was originally L3-5 where the current hardware is." He pointed to the lower spine on the screen. "But L2 and the existing hardware have already begun to degenerate, and the pins have moved, causing more pain." He indicated the neck region. "In his fall that caused the original injury, there was also disc slippage between C6-7. Mr. Santos had wanted to be conservative, so we only did the lower back fusion previously. The cervical region has unfortunately degenerated since then. If we're conservative, we should only need to do a cervical 6-7 anterior cervical discectomy and fusion — that is where we manipulate the slipped disc and fuse the bone there."

"What would you recommend?" She looked at the X-ray closer as he talked.

"There is minor degeneration occurring at thoracic-1 and thoracic-2. I'd include that as well, but it does require more hardware, a bigger incision, and less range of movement after he's healed. But less pain."

Turning to her dad, she pointed to the X-ray. "So, Dad, you have approximately seven cervical vertebrae, twelve thoracic, and five lumbar vertebrae. The doctor will have to work on the lower region again, the lumbar area, and now the neck area." She pointed to the corresponding vertebrae. "What people call the base of the neck, to the upper back. It will be a bigger surgery than last time, with more risks. Doctor, could you go over the risks with us?"

The doctor went over them, going into more detail. When they walked out later, armed with loads of paperwork and follow-ups, her dad thanked her profusely.

"Anak, maybe you should become a doctor!"

"Maybe I should — and take his job!" Carmen said explosively. "Has he never told you any of this?"

Her dad looked sheepish. "I never asked him. His office always gave me these papers to sign, but I never read them."

"Dad, you have to read this stuff! He's cutting into your body. You need to know the risks."

"Aye, as long as I feel better after."

"Has he promised you that too? Because Dad, it's going to hurt after for a while. Hopefully, you'll eventually feel better — but not right away. And there is the very real possibility of nerve damage, which means more pain. The only guarantee is that at first, it's going to hurt worse than it did before and worse than it did the first time. You have to know, too, the pain medication won't work on you as well after all this time."

"We'll talk about it then, Anak. I'm just proud of how smart my daughter is."

Her dad was changing the subject, and she let him with some reluctance. He didn't like talking about the pain medication and his reliance on it. Her mom yelled at him about it often enough.

During her run with Jenny Saturday morning, Carmen mentioned her anxiety about her upcoming group meeting at Logan's.

Bemused, Jenny shook her head. "Girl, you've got it bad for this guy! Just cool it and get to know him a little first."

Carmen, who knew him quite well, or at least knew twenty-seven-year-old Logan well, didn't reply directly to her comment.

"Thanks for the sage advice. I'll take that under advisement."

Laughing, Jenny bumped her shoulder as they ran.

After her run and a quick shower, Carmen agonized over what to wear to her meet-up at Logan's. She finally picked some jeans she'd bought recently and a Something Corporate band shirt, crockedly screen-printed in soneone's garage. Nothing that looked like too much effort. She'd worn that exact outfit to school several times and immediately changed out of it. She threw on a dress, then changed back into the jeans and shirt before decisively closing her closet. Jeans and a shirt. Nothing fancy. Maybe some eyeliner. Yes.

She still had some time to kill, so she got on her computer to chat with her online community.

@Archimedes thanked her for the art she drew for his story and forwarded a list of story recommendations in response. She flagged them for later.

@BearyFunny's message was all exclamation points.

"I won second place!!!! With some edits, they may publish it! Your cover art is killer, too. Can I send them some of your work with the edits?"

Second place? She was happy for @BearyFunny and sent her a quick message congratulating her and telling her the art was hers to send if she wanted.

CHAPTER
10

Carmen parked in front of Logan's place. He still lived in the same home ten years later, so she knew the way, though she'd only been there a handful of times. It was an idyllic stucco and brick home with a white picket fence, perfect grass, and a three-car garage. It wasn't a mansion, but it was a step up from her parents' rundown condo and screamed American suburbia.

Logan's parents divorced when Logan and his older brother were young. Logan lived with his mom until the seventh grade when she and her new husband decided to move to Indonesia. The brothers were forced to live with their dad rather than move a country and language away.

She parked on the sidewalk in front of the home and walked up to the door, glad to see another car already parked. She felt less nervous walking in last.

Logan's stepmom answered. She always wore a matching cardigan and dress, her hair perfectly coiffed.

After polite introductions, she ushered Carmen to the upstairs loft. The room contained a sectional couch, coffee table, and gaming systems. Matching china platters were laid out with snacks.

It felt weird keeping her shoes on. She was afraid of tracking dirt on the plush white carpet, but Mrs. Sardino insisted there was no need to take them off. Despite the threadbare carpet at home, Carmen's mom would yell "Heathen!" at anyone who wore shoes in their condo. Well, she wouldn't scream at guests. She'd just mutter "Hiya!" through gritted teeth to Carmen. Asians did not wear shoes inside. It just wasn't done.

Kelly was already comfortably seated on the floor with her back to the couch and her legs folded under her and to the side. She wore a matching white skirt and collared polo. The pristine Keds on her feet and scrunchie in her hair matched too. Her cheerleading uniform was absent, but her outfit still screamed pep.

As the newcomer, she tried not to let old high school insecurities take root. She remembered that she had talked to Kelly ten years from now, liked her, and witnessed her flirt back with Ganesha. There was no hierarchy of girls with Carmen at the bottom as she had thought or imagined in high school. She was a grown woman, and this was not a competition.

Smiling, she sat across from Logan.

"Love the scrunchie," Carmen said. "If I didn't break every hairband, I'd use them too."

Carmen's mass of hair was too thick and wild for most hair bands, clips, or even scrunchies to tame.

"No, I love your hair! I'm always trying to curl my own, but it never holds." Kelly scrunched up her face, holding out her silky straight ponytail as if offended by it.

"How about me? Any hair advice?" Logan ran a hand across his short, nearly military-cut hair with a laugh.

"Yeah! Grow it out!" Carmen thought of adult Logan's gorgeous wavy black hair.

"No son of mine will be growing his hair out in this house." Logan's dad emerged from the master bedroom down the hall. "You're already in that Lesbian club Logan, I don't need you growing your hair out too."

The comment made Logan grimace. "It's *Thespian*, Dad. And it's the officially accredited title." This looked like an old joke far past its expiration date based on the younger Sardino's facial expression.

Mr. Sardino ignored the correction, turning to the strangers in his home. He was a broad-chested military veteran who always kept his hair strictly military length. "Hello, ladies, nice to meet you."

They introduced themselves and Logan's dad gave Kelly an appraising look.

"This group project of yours looks good in a skirt." He gave his son a wink.

Gross.

The ordinarily confident cheerleader uncharacteristically cleared her throat and subtly pulled her skirt down a fraction.

"Don't be embarrassed. It's just a joke!" He boomed with laughter. "You have fun, Logan." He patted his son hard on the shoulder before heading downstairs. Mr. Sardino was an expert at disguising cruel or offensive comments as comedy.

"Sorry, Kelly, he's..." Logan frowned as if in thought, then gave her a helpless shrug. "Anyway, I came up with some ideas I think should work perfectly." He showed them some chicken scratch in a lined notebook and gave a bemused chuckle at their confused faces. "Okay, I'll just explain it. So, you know the scene on the pirate boat at the end when…"

For almost two hours they worked, laughed, and enjoyed themselves before Carmen realized she needed to head home if she wanted to get ready for work in time. She reluctantly pulled herself away, glowing with happiness at spending quality time with Logan.

Winter break approached quickly with college applications due soon. Conversations at school revolved around where people were applying, last-minute pushes to get grades up, essays, and scholarship submissions. Carmen wasn't too stressed about the process, except for the thought that she might have to go to college again. She didn't hate this second trip through senior year…but she wanted to get back to *her* life. She just wasn't sure how to do that. All Carmen felt she'd accomplished during her few months in 1999 was becoming casual acquaintances with the love of her life and taking a few extra classes.

None of her future knowledge seemed to help in any way. And the more time that passed, the further events diverged. She'd tried new things that her previous self would have never attempted. She'd taken new electives and socialized with different people. And because of these changes, she could no longer predict how things would work out. She reviewed the time travel types again in her head. She was pretty sure she could strike through fixed points too, which only left infinite timelines.

1. ~~Single continuum~~
2. ~~Fixed points~~
3. ~~Time loop~~
4. Infinite timelines

None of this helped her get to her own time though. Where was a time machine when she needed one?

Winter formal was coming up, right after finals and the kick-off for winter break. In an attempt to be feminist or modern, the school made it a Sadie Hawkins deal, so the girls needed to ask the guys. It didn't feel feminist. It felt like added pressure.

She'd taken a women's history class in community college, and they briefly touched on the origin of Sadie Hawkins. It was from a 1930's comic strip about a homely girl named Sadie Hawkins. At 30, she was getting too old to marry, so her father, the mayor, declared November 13th Sadie Hawkins Day. On that day, she played a high-stakes game of tag where the first eligible bachelor she "caught" was legally bound to marry her. Not very feminist and not very nice in reality.

Carmen wanted to ask Logan but found the prospect intimidating. Logan was friendly with her, but she had no illusions about being the only one who might ask him. He was a good-looking guy. But more important than that, he was popular. He headlined every play, he played a sport in a speedo without shame, and for goodness' sake, he was *in a band.* His social capital was a few tax brackets above hers.

During the first dress rehearsal a week before the play, she convinced the props manager to let her show Logan, their Cheshire Cat, the equipment and gear required to pull off the appearing and disappearing trick. He joined her after being fitted for his costume—a dapper three-piece suit in pink and purple stripes, with a ridiculous fluff of pink fur around his face and a widely painted-on grin.

"This isn't what I meant when I said you should grow out your hair, Sardino." She petted his pink fur, and he playfully batted her hand away like a cat.

"Watch it! I got it looking just so, and you're messing it all up." He preened, smoothing his fur back down.

"Oh! I'm sorry! I know how tetchy cats can be."

His sudden hiss surprised a laugh out of her. The costume department had glued oversized fangs onto his prominent canines, giving him a predatory look she found disturbingly attractive.

"I'm kinda into those fangs, Sardino," she said with a half-smile. "You should keep those in."

"Wow... that is very weird."

Instead of responding, she batted at him like a cat. He snickered in return.

"Okay, Tony the Tiger." She steered their playfulness back to the matter at hand with an effort. "We've got work to do! So look here." She pointed to the stage, which still had people working on the last touches. "We came up with what we've proudly dubbed the Cheshire Shuffle, and it will look pretty cool from the audience."

She pointed out the trees they made with a ladder and a perch for him to sit on. There were three in total—one in the foreground on the left, a smaller one further back on the right, and the smallest one on the left again. The size difference created the illusion of a long forest path with trees disappearing into the distance.

Logan would sit in the first with a spotlight on him. When he 'disappeared,' the spotlight would turn off, and he would duck out of sight. Another person in costume in the next tree would pop up onto their ledge before the spotlight lit up the body double. A speaker would emit Logan's voice from the other tree while the tree furthest from the audience contained a neon Cheshire Cat face with another speaker. This would give the appearance of the Cheshire Cat magically teleporting from tree to tree.

"This is going to look so cool!" he said. "Show me the perch and the harness equipment."

On the stage, she directed him to the first tree. She fitted him with the harness, painted pink and purple with a furry tail he could play with attached to the back. It tethered him to the safety equipment since his perch wasn't very wide.

Carmen would be hidden behind the tree the entire time, helping him up and off his ledge when the cue came. She would also be in charge of making sure his equipment was hooked up correctly. She and her partner, who would be helping the second Cheshire Cat, watched videos on safety and equipment a week prior in preparation.

She demonstrated how to sling the rope through the safety carabiner and the proper knots. "I'll be doing the tie-off for you, but I want you to know what it should look like. All safety equipment should get a two-person sign-off." Adult Carmen dabbled in rock climbing. Not a lot, she didn't have the nerves for it. But she'd done enough to know all this before it was taught to her for the play.

"So, I'll be doing a figure eight double loop." She tied it slowly for him. "I like mine to lie just so." She pointed to how the double figure eight should lie. "Because I don't like it looking messy. Also, the carabiner should always be locked. You check it by doing this." She pushed on the carabiner gate to show the lock was in place.

"I trust you." He smiled, baring cosmetically lengthened canines.

"You shouldn't, Garfield. It's your neck on the line." She tried to keep a straight face, but the ends of her lips kept curling up in amusement.

"Here." She handed him the harness. "Put it on, and let's do a quick practice run before we start dress rehearsal."

She helped Logan into the harness and tightened the various leg loops. She had to get a little too close to his pelvis to get it done, and they both twittered with nervous laughter.

"I usually save second base for the third date."

"Ha. Ha. You try getting this equipment on without my help." She tugged on his leg loop until it was unnecessarily tight.

"Mercy, I'll do what you say." He held his hands up in surrender.

"That's what I thought."

"I like a strong woman. Hey, you are just full of strange knowledge, aren't you? First, you know cheers in every language and, like, the history of Eastern Europe or whatever, then you know all this safety equipment. I should start calling you Trivial Pursuit instead of Ramen." He pulled at one of her curls. She blushed bright red.

"You should be glad they made me learn this safety equipment, or you'd be on your own, Oliver."

"Oliver?"

"Like from Oliver and Company?"

"You couldn't think of a better cartoon cat? I like these nicknames, Trivia." He winked at her. "But I think you can do better. Oliver, really?"

His oversized canines made another appearance, his grin ferocious. She melted at his look.

They completed a few test runs and she quizzed him

on the equipment as they refastened it multiple times. In nursing school, they had a technique they called the teach-back-and-show-me. She used it on her patients all the time. She would show them a task a few times, like how to check their glucose, then make them show her and teach it back to her. It was a great trick to make the information stick.

"Okay, Trivia, then I push here to make sure you locked it." He pushed on the carabiner gate.

"Oh! Was there ever a cat so clever as magical Mr. Mistoffelees!" she said in a singsong voice, her off-pitch tone giving unintentional added humor to the line. His eyebrows went up, a surprised and impressed huff of a laugh escaping him.

"Trivia. Really? *Cats*?"

"Well, you insulted my last reference. I dug deep for that one."

"Color me impressed."

Their eyes met and held as they grinned at each other. There was always something so intimidating and intimate about staring into someone's eyes. But she stared into Logan's familiar eyes, brownish green with the edges always crinkled in laughter. Many of the details of his face were off — no facial hair emphasized his square jaw, no curling shoulder-length hair — but the eyes were the same.

Now would be the perfect time to ask him to the dance. Just as she worked up her courage, a loud clap called their attention away to the front of the room. Mrs. Malone stood at the foot of the stage.

"Okay, kids, to your places," she said, her hands still held together from clapping them. "I think we're going to get this rehearsal started from the top before it gets

too far past dinnertime, and your parents start calling."
Mrs. Malone looked a little frazzled, her hair escaping
its customary ponytail. "Carmen, Julianna—pull your
trees into the wings. We'll start with Act One, Scene One
props. Where's our Alice? Are you in costume yet? That
wig looks all wrong under these lights. You sure you
won't dye your hair?"

Carmen and Logan gave each other parting grins
before splitting up for their Act One roles.

During her Saturday morning run Carmen told Jenny all
about Logan.

"He does not sound uninterested. You should ask
him."

"Yeah, I just don't want to do it in the halls or after
class. It feels weird and too public. I'm going to ask him
on Thursday, the first night of the play. If he says no, it'll
be awkward, but at least I can ask him in private."

Carmen's weekend routine carried her through
work, homework, and chores around the house. As was
customary, she, Josie, and Ganesha went out on Sunday
night for burgers and a movie.

Mattias, still working the weekend concessions stand,
grinned at them when they got in line for snacks.

"Hey! I got tickets to the last night of the play," he
said when they reached the front of the line. "My buddy
Diego is the White Rabbit, and I promised him I wouldn't
miss it."

"Nice! I'm not in this play," Carmen said. "But check
out the Cheshire Cat scene. My team engineered that."

"Will do!" There was a cough from the person behind
them in the concession line. They moved off to the side
and got their popcorn from another person as Mattias

94

took the next person's order, waving to them as they walked to their theater.

"You've become a chatty Cathy, haven't you?" Ganesha cut her eyes to Carmen.

"He's friendly. I'm friendly. Nothing else to say."

"Mmmhmmm," Josie said in a singsong voice.

CHAPTER 11

Carmen barely had a spare moment to consider asking Logan to the dance all week. It was the week of the play and the week before Thanksgiving. After that, they would only have a week of school left, finals, and the dance before winter break. Her dad's surgery was scheduled for the first weekend of the break then her grandmother would fly in for the holidays. She looked forward to seeing her grandmother again. The last time she lived this year, Carmen had mainly kept to herself and barely spent any time with her grandmother when she visited. Her grandmother would pass away a few short years from then, and Carmen had hardly known her. She didn't plan on making that same mistake.

The first night of the play rolled in before she knew it. With everyone caught up in last-minute preparations, she barely saw Logan until the play was already underway. When Logan's turn to get into position for the Cheshire Shuffle came, she hunched behind the tree prop with him and tied off his equipment, making him check the gate and his rope.

When it was nearly his cue, she whispered, "Good luck Sylvester, don't break a leg." He climbed his ladder and stole the show. He swirled with motion, first flamboyantly draping himself across his perch, then sitting up with crossed legs, then preening his tail and head mane. He delivered his lines in this funny drawling, purring voice. He affected a French accent with overdone rolling Rs and long Os. When it came time for his disappearing and reappearing act through the trees, the spotlight went out, and she helped him duck back behind his prop as the other Cheshire Cat got into position.

The spotlight lit up the other cat seamlessly with only a moment between spotlights. The crowd gasped and murmured appreciatively, then Logan started to sing his exit song.

Grinning at her, he sang the first repeating verse, which she could hear from his close proximity, though it came through the speakers under the silent body double across the stage.

> "Twas Brillig
> And the slithy toves
> Did gyre and gimble in the wabe
> All Mimsy were the borogroves
> And the mome raths outgrabe."

The light went out on the silent body double. A beat later, the stage went dark except for the lit-up oversized Cheshire face with a moving mouth that grinned maniacally down on a frightened Alice.

Logan repeated his line but whispered, so it came out

breathy and deliciously creepy. When he finished, they both wore grins from a scene done right. She knew she couldn't let the moment pass. There was only a short break between sets where they had to rush the tree prop off stage and move to the next act.

"Hey... so this maybe isn't the best time, but has anyone asked you to Sadie Hawkins?"

His expression dropped, and she instantly knew someone already had.

"Sorry, Trivia, Kelly asked me..."

"Oh!" Her face heated with embarrassment. "I didn't realize you guys were dating —"

"We're not! I mean, she asked me, and we're going together..."

Mrs. Malone whisper-shouted at them. "Get that prop off the stage before the lights go on, Carmen. Logan, you're needed in wardrobe!"

They scrambled away to their roles.

She should have asked earlier! Ugh, not that there was any guarantee he would have said yes! Just because he liked her in ten years didn't mean a thing here in high school. She didn't get another chance to talk to him that night, not that she wanted to.

Despondent, she got home late looking for a distraction. Adult Carmen would have drowned her heartache in a glass of wine and a chick-flick, but there was no alcohol in this house. So she dug through the freezer for the rocky road ice cream and drowned her sorrows in another kind of pint.

CHAPTER 12

On the second night of the play, Carmen checked Logan's equipment in silence, the air stale and awkward between them.

Clearing his throat, Logan spoke to fill the unnatural silence. "Don't let me fall now that I've said yes to someone else."

Uncomfortable that he acknowledged the elephant in the room, she smiled at the weak joke. "You don't know that I was asking you. I just asked if someone *else* had asked you."

"Not that I wouldn't have minded you asking."

She could tell he was trying to make eye contact with her, but she felt guilty for flirting with him. He was going with someone else to the dance. And even if she felt some sort of way about it, she wasn't going to *make eyes* at someone else's date, especially when she liked Kelly.

An idea lit up in her mind. She knew someone *else* who showed an interest in Kelly. Or would eventually.

It was a minor thing that Ganesha wouldn't flirt openly with Kelly for ten more years...

Tightening her smile, she tugged at Logan's rope with perhaps a bit too much force, wishing things were different.

He played his part just as brilliantly as the night before, and the rest of the play raced by with no other chances to talk.

The next and last night, they had their usual banter while she checked his gear.

"I think you should steal this suit, wear it to the winter formal. It really brings out your eyes."

"First, you're into my fangs, and now you're into this suit? I'm starting to question your taste Trivia, that's kinky." He bared his fangs.

"Whatever." She affected a bored expression, turning her nose up at him. "You're so basic."

"Excuse me?" He drew back, a confused quirk playing along his lips.

Was basic not a common term yet? She failed to recall where or when the slang came from. "I'm sorry," she said, rushing to explain and not wanting to offend. "It's not an insult. It just means you like boring things?" She winced, the explanation worse than the slang.

"Still sounds like an insult..." He looked puzzled as he climbed the ladder.

Once he was out of sight, she smacked herself in the head. Most of the time, the differences between 1999 and 2009 were unnoticeable. Other times, it was like navigating a foreign language.

The final act ended before she knew it. The play was type-two fun—a ton of work but satisfying when everything came together. There were minor mishaps, missed cues, and forgotten or winged lines, but on the whole, Society put together a play to be proud of.

They all queued up for their last-night bows. As the actors marched off stage, Carmen linked arms with her fellow prop makers in preparation to march out for their applause.

Paraded onto the stage with the others, the glaring lights turned the audience dark. Carmen narrowed her eyes to slits, trying to make out Josie, Ganesha, and maybe Mattias in the audience. But a glint of metal off to the far left in the audience caught her eye. There was a wheelchair with a young girl... Carmen squinted to get a better look and caught the girl's wide eyes staring back, her mouth open in shock.

Carmen's face slackened in surprise too. The girl signed the letter C combined with the sign for noodles — Carmen's sign name—and tilted her head in question. Carmen nodded once at her, but before she could do much more than that, she was ushered off the stage for the lighting, music, and costume crew to make their bows.

Carmen tried to break formation and take another look at the audience, but her crew still had their arms linked with hers and pulled her away. Then the stage manager told them to break down and store the more costly equipment before they could join their families and friends in the audience.

By the time she reached the audience seating, the crowd was up and milling about or leaving. She didn't see a wheelchair anywhere.

A loud call of "Carmen!" came from behind, and Mattias ambushed her and congratulated her on the night's success.

"Yo, that thing with the cat, and the lights, and the spooky poem was dope!"

"Thanks," she said, still looking around.

"Ramen! Good job!" Ganesha and Josie crowded around her too.

"Thanks! I wasn't even in the play," she said, abashed at the outpouring of praise.

"Well, that is true. Never mind. I take it back," Ganesha deadpanned.

"I don't!" Josie said. "The Cheshire Shuffle or whatever you told us about was just as cool as promised."

Carmen's attention turned fully to them, her earlier seed of an idea coalescing into a plan.

"It was a group effort," Carmen said in response to Josie, then turned to Mattias. "But hey, I wanted to ask, would you go to the Sadie Hawkins with me?"

A pleased expression flashed across his face. "Oh! Actually, yeah, that sounds awesome!"

"Let's go as a group, as friends?" Carmen said in a rush. "Josie, Ganesha? You guys too?"

Josie quirked up a blonde brow in good humor. "What, you're asking all of us now? I should tell you that polygamy is illegal in California."

"Come on! Let's get dressed up and go have some fun."

"I'm in," Josie said.

Then Carmen and Josie turned to Ganesha with pleading looks.

"What? I'm not your mom. You don't need my permission to go." Ganesha crossed her arms.

"Let's go 'Nesha!" Carmen said in a needling voice. "It'll be a good time."

"Fine." Ganesha rolled her eyes heavenward. "But I'm no one's date."

Carmen linked arms with her. "How 'bout we're all your date?"

That got another look of exaggerated annoyance, but the tilt at the edge of her mouth said she was pleased to be included.

Once Carmen returned home that night, she stayed up late, too keyed up thinking over the implications to fall asleep.

The girl she'd tried to save at the reunion was there, *recognized her*, and signed her name. She'd only interacted with the girl in a dream, possibly a dream they both remembered. So, the girl must have been thrown back in time too?

Carmen logged online and tried to do some snooping. She didn't know the girl's name, but maybe she could find information through Mrs. Malone? Carmen didn't even know Mrs. Malone's first name...

She dug through an old yearbook after some thought. Joanne. Okay, so she had a first and last name. After an hour of fruitless searching, Carmen gave up. There wasn't anything else besides a brief mention on Jamboree High's website. Pre-social media and the early internet were annoyingly private.

She now needed to double down on getting to know Mrs. Malone so she could speak with her daughter. Maybe Carmen had been thrown back in time to help save Mrs. Malone somehow, even though she had no idea how to stop someone from having a stroke. It couldn't be a coincidence that the other girl was also somehow a time traveler. If there was any rhyme or reason to this, the two had to have something to do with why Carmen was in 1999 instead of 2009.

Finally getting into bed, Carmen stared at the ceiling in thought and revisited the plan she started to formulate during the play. She made it pretty clear to Mattias that she was only interested in going as friends. She knew that future Ganesha was into Kelly. She thought Mattias and Josie's humor matched well with each other. She already knew who Josie would end up with in the future. But a small high school fling couldn't hurt if the timeline was already changed beyond repair. And that cleared the way for her and Logan to let chemistry do its thing. Hopefully.

She was going to play a little matchmaking.

CHAPTER 13

Now that *Alice in Wonderland* was over, Society moved on to preparations for *Peter Pan*. Carmen read through the script, anticipating the upcoming tryouts. She was determined to spend more time around Logan. If she were in the cast, they would have practice in common too. She had missed her chance to ask him to the dance partly because they only talked when their paths crossed, which wasn't as often as she liked.

After some deliberation, she decided to try out for Tiger Lily's part. Carmen knew, due to her future knowledge, that Logan would play as Hook. Very little of Carmen's future knowledge came in handy, but at least this did. Tiger Lily only delivered about six lines, as she spent the majority of her stage time tied up as Hook's hostage. Kinky. Plus, she wasn't keen on playing a major role, but wanted to spend as much time with Logan as possible. Low pressure, high gains.

Still, anxiety had her picking at her lunch, stage fright

filling her with dread. And she only needed to deliver her lines today in front of Society, not the whole school! When she showed up at Society later that day, she joined the group of students reading lines in a quiet circle. Logan paced with his script, mouthing the words to himself and dramatically waving his hand about. When he spotted her, he beckoned her over.

"Trivia! Are you trying out?"

"Yeah... I decided to try out for Tiger Lily, but I hope I have no competition or I'm sunk. How about you?"

"I'm hoping for Hook, but I know a couple of people are interested." He subtly gestured to another classmate who sat hunched over a script, muttering the words under his breath.

"What scene are you doing?"

"I was thinking about doing the scene we changed up for our class final, but you know — without the gore and mayhem. I heard a rumor —"

"Hello!" Mrs. Malone called out to the scattered students, interrupting what Logan was about to say. "Before we start tryouts and set planning and everything, I'd like to tell you about a special opportunity first. For finals in theater class this semester, we're doing play rewrites. I asked all classes to remix, change, or modernize a classic scene from a play. I've enjoyed this prompt so much, I'd like you guys — in groups if need be — to come up with a way to change *Peter Pan* in a subtle but interesting way. And if it's a good enough idea, we'll change our public performance to accommodate. This won't come into effect until next semester, but if you have a good enough idea, I will also feature you as a co-creator in the play program."

The class exploded into conversation. This piqued many of the seniors' and some junior students' attention.

Many kids in Society planned on going to competitive theater programs for college and would love anything they could add to pad their college applications.

"Listen, I know you're excited." Mrs. Malone waved her hands, silencing the room. "I'll give you a few minutes to talk, then we're moving on to tryouts. We'll talk about proposals as soon as we come back from break."

Carmen turned to Logan, who smiled at her. "I heard a rumor we'd get extra credit if we come up with a good enough change to Peter Pan. I really liked our idea for finals — do you think it's too much?"

"Kinda?" Carmen said reluctantly. "The keyword being subtle. Killing off Hook and making Peter Pan a murderer is fun shock value in class, but performing it in front of the whole school and our families? We'd have to give trigger warnings, or like, rate it PG-13. Parental guidance strongly advised."

He looked thoughtful. "You've got a point there. It's not exactly family-friendly…"

"Listen, I'm still down for brainstorming ideas together. I was reading the script, and I forgot how offensive the whole 'picaninny' tribe is." The song called 'What Makes the Red Man red' was just…wrong. "Instead of using some offensive made-up Native American tribe, we could just…take those scenes out? They're not necessary to the plot anyway."

"Aren't you trying out for Tiger Lily? Wouldn't that erase you from the story?"

"Yeah, that would suck." Carmen tapped her finger against her lip in thought. "And she's kind of vital to the story, I think. She's like — the example of how bad Hook can be since he kidnaps her. Maybe…maybe we could base it on a real tribe? Like, Australian Aboriginals or —

Ooh! Or like Hawaiian natives! Or Filipinos! I know a little bit about Filipino history!"

His gaze was fond. "Of course you do, Trivia. You know a little bit about everything." Carmen glowed under his praise before schooling her expression. Was this flirting? Was he flirting? Mrs. Malone called for attention again and for tryouts to start.

The following week went by quickly, but she never got a chance to speak with Mrs. Malone about her daughter. She had work and school, and then it was Thanksgiving weekend. She dreaded holidays with her family. Holidays in the Santos home never turned out as they did in the movies. Thanksgiving wasn't even a holiday Filipinos got excited over. Filipinos were all about Christmas — the lights, the nativity scene, the decorations. Heck, her family was from the literal Christmas Capital of the Philippines. It was what her native hometown was known for. Christmas was in their blood.

On Thanksgiving, she helped her mom make chicken adobo instead of turkey. They used soy sauce, vinegar, garlic, and various unlabeled seasoning mixes from some auntie back home. After she and her mom finished prepping the adobo and placing it on the stove to simmer, her mom guilted her into decorating for Christmas. She dreaded this part. Her mom always wanted things just so but inevitably became frustrated at Carmen or her dad halfway through the process.

"Aye, you're being too rough with those boxes. You'll break the glass inside. *NO!*"

Standing on a precarious ladder, Carmen pulled decorations from the attic space and almost dropped the box in surprise, barely righting herself and the package in time.

"*Hay nako*, not you Anak, your dad. No, do not take your pain pill yet. It isn't time."

"Yes, it is, look—" he pointed to the clock. It was five minutes to the hour. He popped them in his mouth and swallowed them dry.

"No, I'm sure you took them only three hours ago."

"I know when I took it."

"Well, did you take it three hours ago or four?"

Her dad paused. "The pain doctor said I could take it every three hours."

"That pain doctor is a scam artist. He just wants more money. He doesn't care if you're a drug addict." She hissed the last part.

Her dad labored to push himself up from the couch where he'd been enjoying a mug of tea.

"Yeah, go! Run away! You're useless anyway..." Her mom devolved into muttered Tagalog.

Her dad shuffled to the bedroom and shut the door.

"If he wants to be an addict, fine," her mom muttered angrily. "But when your lola comes next week, I don't want him to embarrass me."

"Just leave him alone, Mom." Carmen sighed, long-suffering. "He's having surgery in two weeks."

"You're always on his side. Do you care that he does nothing? You love him more than me, and I'm the one who takes care of you, feeds you, and pays the bills! You're so ungrateful. Here give me that." She snatched the box away from her. "You have to be careful."

Carmen rolled her eyes and took a deep breath, letting it out slowly. She wanted to walk away too, but this was something they did as a family. She needed to stick around and help decorate. They both kneeled on the ground and opened the first box. They started taking out each ornament from its nest of paper towels—their cheap packing material of choice. Inside were dozens of ornaments made of wood and glass, paper and metal. It was a hodgepodge of ornaments their family had collected over the years from garage sales and secondhand shops, as well as a few coveted elementary school ones made of macaroni or popsicle sticks. Carmen placed a few ornaments on the tree, but her mom moved them as soon as she turned to pick another out.

"You're putting them in the wrong place. Here."

"How can I be putting them in the wrong place? We've got a whole tree to cover."

"No, there's branches missing here. I have to cover it." She moved another ornament several inches over, to a non-existent bare spot. Her mom frowned at the tree.

"If your dad worked, we could get a new tree." She shook her head, a wrinkle between her brows. The tree was an old green plastic Carmen had seen her whole life. The pre-lit lights had stopped working ages ago. Carmen realized she hadn't seen any lights yet, so she stood to search for them.

Her mom threw her hands in the air. "Are you leaving now, too? Do I have to do everything myself?" she said in a nasty tone.

"Stop being dramatic." Carmen pointed to the ladder she was now at the base of, lifting one brow at her. "I'm looking for the box with the lights."

"Don't call me dramatic! I'm your mother, you have to show some respect."

Ignoring her tone, Carmen climbed the ladder instead.

Her mom stood directly under her. "I said, show some respect, Carmen. I'm not going to accept your attitude."

"Yeah, mom, okay," she said in a placating voice, intentionally staying even toned. "I'm going to grab the lights."

"I think I wrapped them around a paper towel roll last year."

Carmen peered around the attic space, finding boxes of old clothes and photos, but no paper towel roll. She shoved aside a few bins and found another box labeled "Christmas."

"Aye, just come down, I'll look," her mom said, tone impatient.

"Hold on, I found another box."

"Hand it down."

"I got it," Carmen said, grabbing the box to pull it out. As she stepped down the ladder, juggling the large box, her mom snatched it, but the box slipped and hit the bottom rung of the ladder with a foreboding crunch.

"Hey! I said be careful!" her mom yelled, bending to pick up the box. The sound of tinkling broken glass could be heard inside.

Carmen's thinning patience ran out and her tone turned shrill. "Stop being such a nightmare!"

"No one in this house respects me!" her mom screamed back.

"That's because you're miserable to be around!"

Reaching her limit, Carmen stepped off the ladder and stormed out of the living room, the tree only half-decorated.

Her mom threw an ornament down the hall after her. "Yeah, fine! Go! You're all useless!"

Carmen slammed her door and locked it.

A moment later, her parents' raised voices filtered through the walls from their bedroom. It wasn't even 4 p.m. yet. A crash sounded and the yelling grew louder.

She could not stay in this house another moment. She would likely start breaking things too. She paced her room, her hands in her hair, then sat at her computer to vent. No one was on AOL Instant Messenger, so she got on her journal instead.

> "I HATE the holidays, and I hate my mom, and I hate this house. Other people get to have family gatherings around the fireplace and drink hot cocoa and play music, or whatever it is happy families do. My family? We scream at each other and break things. Why do people put so much pressure on each other to have a "Happy Holiday?" Do you know what I want? Some peace and QUIET."

Josie's avatar popped up as available on AOL. Carmen saved her journal entry and messaged her friend.

> @missAnthropic: I'm con-templating burning my house down. Stop me?

> @CozyJosie: I'll visit you in prison, I promise.

> @missAnthropic: What are you doing? I need to get out of here.

> @CozyJosie: My mom is at work, so nothing. I'll call Ganesha. Let's meet at

Pirate Park in 15 minutes.

Leaving a note on the fridge, Carmen escaped through the front door before either of her parents could stop her. When she arrived at the park, Josie sat alone on the swing set.

Her friend was bundled up against the cool weather in a bright red chunky sweater and jeans, a blonde ponytail poking out of a mismatched pink and green pom-pom beanie. Josie could be five or twenty-five, but her aesthetic would always prioritize comfort and function over fashion.

"Ganesha is still finishing up eating with her family," Josie said in lieu of a greeting. "But she said she'd meet us in an hour. Promised us samosas."

Carmen perked up. She hadn't eaten the adobo she and her mom had made at home and felt her mouth water. Ganesha always complained about her overcrowded home, but the food was plentiful and amazing.

Josie's look was measured. "Want to talk about what's turned you into a pyromaniac?"

"Am I a pyromaniac if I haven't lit anything on fire?"

"I'll take that as a no, then." Josie dug her toe into the sand, before changing topics. "So, I'm curious… When you asked Mattias to the dance, you made it pretty clear you wanted to go as friends. I'm just surprised. You were kind of obsessed with him all summer."

No reason to dodge the truth. "I've got this thing for Logan."

"The guy from your theater class? Really? He's kind of…"

"I know, he's popular," Carmen said, filling in her pause.

"No. Yeah. Well, he's just kind of the all-American type.

I didn't think you'd be into that?" Josie absentmindedly twirled her ponytail.

Carmen gave the comment some thought. "I came to this realization," she said slowly, looking up at the gray sky. "That people are just *people*, you know."

"Well, that's crystal clear." Josie raised her left eyebrow as if to say, 'go on?'

"No. I mean that we're graduating in a year. Right? No one will care who was popular in high school. These labels don't *mean* anything. You know, we're all going to graduate and become adults and live life. You know? Like, you'll be this super-successful lawyer, I'm sure." She was sure. "And who cares if you were in the Model UN and weren't a cheerleader and didn't have a high school boyfriend or whatever. Social status in high school doesn't matter."

"Flattery will get you everywhere."

Carmen returned to the topic about Logan. "He's in my drama class, and he's really passionate about it. And he's funny. And he's thoughtful. I feel happy when I'm around him. That's why I like him."

She couldn't say they fit together because they were already together in some future iteration. But she was finding she didn't need to. She liked this version she'd gotten to know too.

"Awww." Josie's expression turned saccharine. "You really like him! Why didn't you ask him to the dance?"

"Oh, God." Carmen buried her face in her hands. "I did, and it was so embarrassing. Someone already asked him. And they're going together! But, I think, as friends...I kind of have a plan..."

Debating how much to tell Josie, Carmen looked around the still empty playground. "I'm going to tell you something, but you can't say anything, okay?"

"Promise."

"So, I think Ganesha might be, you know, um…" Carmen vaguely waved her hand about. She had second thoughts at Josie's blank face.

"You know!" Carmen gave Josie a look, which she returned with raised eyebrows.

"I have no idea what you're talking about."

"Okay, have you ever known Ganesha to be into guys?"

"Yeah, she likes Adam in our AP History class." Josie looked like she might be catching on to what Carmen was trying to say and frowned at Carmen.

"No, you think Adam is super cute, and she said she does too."

Josie sighed. "I mean, Adam is pretty much the perfect male form, so why wouldn't she?"

"Yeah, but she's never shown any interest in guys. She's never dated."

"So what?" Josie had a stubborn frown across her lightly freckled face. "You've never dated anyone. I've never dated anyone. Are you a lesbian?"

"Look, just, believe me. Kelly and 'Nesha will hit it off."

Josie didn't look convinced, but they both spotted Ganesha walking up the path from the parking lot with Tupperware in hand and waving at them.

"Don't tell her I said any of this, okay?" Carmen said with a quiet undertone.

"Of course," Josie said, still frowning at her.

They snacked on the samosas Ganesha promised and chatted for the rest of the evening. Carmen went home to a quiet living room, the half-decorated Christmas tree

117

and broken ornaments the only testament to the earlier fight. She pulled the adobo out of the fridge and ate it straight out of the Tupperware.

That weekend, just before finals, Carmen met up with Logan and Kelly to rehearse their skit for their theater final.

When Carmen went upstairs, Kelly and Logan already sat comfortably on the couch. This time Kelly sat next to Logan with her legs up and sock-covered feet touching Logan's thigh. There wasn't another seat available on the couch, as Kelly and Logan had spread out their stuff — and Kelly's legs — across the sofa. So, Carmen sat across from them in a chair. Kelly kept flipping her hair, laughing at Logan's jokes, and poking him with her foot. The blatant flirting made Carmen want to hit something.

Kelly and Logan chatted with her the entire time, and they concentrated mainly on schoolwork. But Kelly was definitely looking for more than just a date to Winter Formal. Carmen just…didn't have it in her to compete for a guy. Even Logan. It made her feel…tight and ugly inside. She hoped her plan at the dance worked out before anything more than flirting happened…

She hated every foot touch and coquettish hair flip. She hated that her jaw clenched every time a touch lingered between them. She hated most of all how it made her feel. Why was she in the past? She had thought it might be to figure out if she should say yes to Logan's proposal, but she was starting to think it was just to torture her.

Carmen only stayed long enough to run through their parts, then made her excuses and left for home.

Finals week was excruciating. She thought she left school behind her when she graduated from nursing school, and yet there she was, having to take exams.

Thursday was their theater final. Mrs. Malone unexpectedly called out sick and left a substitute in charge with a clunky video recorder on a tripod so she could grade their finals over winter break. Since this was the last class before winter break, Carmen had lost her chance to talk to Mrs. Malone about her daughter before the spring semester started.

Dressed in simple costumes for their theater final, Carmen wore a pirate hat and a red jacket. Logan was dressed head to toe in green as Peter Pan, and Kelly dressed as Wendy in a white dress and big red hair bow.

They got a few claps but mostly shocked silence when they finished.

One student looked faintly sick. "Well...I was not expecting that."

Another classmate said, "The fake blood was certainly...believable?"

"Well..." the substitute mumbled, "you effectively turned a children's story into horror. Congratulations."

Logan, as a blood-splattered Peter Pan, cackled maniacally, still playing his role as a killer with panache.

CHAPTER 14

Friday being a half-day gave Carmen plenty of time to prepare for the dance. She and her friends had gone shopping, but the cost of most traditional formalwear had been too steep for Carmen, so she "shopped" in her friends' closets. Carmen found a cropped boxy pink Sari top in Ganesha's sister's closet that fit her and paired it with a pink tulle skirt she picked up at Goodwill. She was going full Sarah Jessica Parker. She'd recently seen an episode of *Sex and the City*, and the intro inspired her. She also picked up some purple hair dye to go with her pink dress.

Her mom? Not so impressed with the look.

"Oh *hiya*, what have you done to your hair?"

"It will wash out, don't worry." In ten to twelve washes, the box said.

"What is this you're wearing?" Her mom gestured, then tried to pull at her top.

"It's fashion, Mom. I promise." Carmen pushed her

hand away.

"It looks ridiculous."

"Have you seen *Sex and the City*?"

"*What* in the city? What are you watching? This doesn't sound like appropriate television for a seventeen-year-old girl."

"It's a popular TV show. It's not porn or anything."

"Don't use that word!" Her mom screeched.

"It's not a bad word, *Mom*."

It didn't matter that Carmen was twenty-seven years old on the inside, her mom would always bring the teenage drama queen out of her. Carmen slouched and crossed her arms defensively, sighing loudly.

"Aye, just pull the skirt up. Your stomach is showing! Why is that shirt so short?" Carmen obliged with reluctance, hiking the skirt up high to cover her bare stomach.

She drove to Josie's, the plan being that the three of them and Mattias would meet there before driving to the dance together. Josie's mom answered the door and was still in uniform, having just gotten off her shift.

Josie's dad had passed away when she was a toddler, leaving her pregnant mom scrambling for a way to support a young family. Ms. O'Connell put herself through paramedic school, still grieving her partner. She was hardly ever around because she worked as much overtime as possible, but each kid had their own room and always provided everything they needed.

"Hi honey, don't you look cute? I'm getting Carrie in New York, running for the subway vibe, right? I just love the ballerina skirt." She also tried to be the "cool mom."

"On the nose Ms. O'Connell," Carmen said with a wink.

"It's perfect. I wish I'd been able to shop with you guys." Ms. O'Connell said the next part in a conspiratorial tone. "I'm not a huge fan of what my girl picked out, but don't tell her that."

"I heard you!" said a voice from the staircase.

"I'm sorry, honey, it's just so frumpy!" Ms. O'Connell winced.

Carmen spotted Josie at the top of the stairs. She wore a fitted three-quarter-length sleeved dress in a red, brown, and orange knit pattern. She'd braided her hair in a lot of tiny braids and woven in ribbons, which framed her small face. It was a '70s vibe from head to toe, worn with heeled knee-high brown boots to complete the look.

"No, Ms. O'Connell. It's a whole mood, and I love it."

"I guess it's true what they say — all fashion is cyclical. I was just hoping we would skip the decade of bell-bottoms and crochet." The older woman sighed.

"Come on." Josie waved Carmen up. "I'm just finishing 'Nesha's hair." She stared once Carmen came closer. "Speaking of hair, I like the purple!"

Entering her friend's room, she was bombarded by clothes flung on every flat surface, evidence of their efforts to get ready. Ganesha sat before the vanity, wearing a blue dress with capped sleeves. She never saw seventeen-year-old Ganesha in anything other than jeans and T-shirts, so it was a welcome surprise.

"Love the dress. When I came over, I didn't see that in your sisters' closets, or I'd have borrowed it."

Ganesha didn't move, concentrating on French-braiding her black hair. "It's her mom's." She gestured to Joise with her elbow. "She made me put it on when I got here. We're about the same size, and she hated what I was wearing." She caught sight of Carmen through the mirror

123

and whipped around. "Love the hair, hate the outfit."

"Did I ask your opinion?"

"You're still friends with me, and I'm opinionated. So?" Ganesha shrugged and turned back to the mirror to finish her hair.

Carmen snorted.

The doorbell rang, and then Ms. O'Connell, sounding perplexed, yelled up the stairs. "You're um... You three, your date is here."

When they paraded downstairs, Mattias stood in a dress shirt, pants, and suspenders in the doorway. He cut his mohawk down to an inch and dyed it highlighter orange. He held out three corsages, grinning widely. He wore a brand-new septum piercing, his visage reminding Carmen of Ferdinand the bull—a mean-looking animal with a heart of gold. Mattias was all punk rock on the outside and marshmallows inside.

"Looking good, ladies! I didn't know what colors you guys would be wearing, so I got them—" He gestured to the flowers. "—all in yellow. You know, like the color of friendship." His grin grew wider still.

Okay, that was just saccharine sweet. If Logan didn't totally consume her heart and mind, she'd be interested in him for that gesture alone.

They all piled into his old green station wagon with faux wood paneling across the side. He drove like he looked, with music loud, windows open, and too fast. When they squealed into the parking lot, they were all a little windswept and breathless. He brandished a flask after parking toward the back of the lot.

"I have whiskey with me. Do you guys want some now? I've got soda too." He dug around in the glove box, pulling out a bottle of Coca-Cola in triumph.

Ganesha's sip of the whiskey looked small. Or, knowing Ganesha, she more likely pretended to take a sip. Josie took a few gulps of the whiskey, then swigged some Coke before offering the flask to Carmen. She took a measured sip, determinedly remaining clear-headed to execute her matchmaking plan.

The twinkle lights and blue and white shimmery foil on the walls transformed the space inside. Carmen craned her neck to see over the crowd, trying to spot Logan and Kelly in the bustle of students. Luckily, she spotted them with mutual friends. Diego, who was both Mattias's best friend and the White Rabbit in their last play, stood next to Logan, heads thrown back in laughter. Perfect. She could start step one of her plan.

"Hey Mattias, there's Diego."

Noticing Diego, Mattias waved. It wasn't a highly complex plan. She just needed to get various groups to hang out together, and hopefully, chemistry would do its thing.

"Is it cool if we hang with Diego?" Mattias said, changing directions to head toward Diego.

"Yeah, of course!"

They were all in various semi-formal to formal wear, with Kelly wearing a strapless red dress that matched the red tie Logan was wearing with his dress pants and shirt. Logan and Kelly's faces lit up when they saw Carmen, and she felt briefly guilty for wanting the guy Kelly came here with. Kelly was just so friendly! Harder to dislike someone who liked her.

Carmen made introductions, though they'd attended school together for years. "This is Ganesha and Josie, my best friends."

Mattias fist-bumped Diego in greeting. Logan lit up in

recognition, speaking to Carmen's best friends.

"I think you guys are in my AP History class," he said. "How'd you do on that final? It was a beeaaaast."

This devolved into talk about exams. Carmen noted with cautious hope that Kelly and Logan weren't holding hands. Carmen turned to Kelly, drawing her into the conversation and hoping to lure her away from Logan too.

"I think we nailed the theater final," she said. "You played the horrified witness perfectly."

"Yeah, I mean, once everyone recovered from the shock." She flipped her long flat-ironed hair over one shoulder in affected pride.

"We may have overdone it with the fake blood," Carmen said, conceding. "The first row was like the splash zone at SeaWorld!"

They both cackled, sharing satisfaction over pulling off their shocking finale. Observing Ganesha standing by but not participating in Josie and Logan's conversation, Carmen searched for a subject to pull her into theirs. She needed Kelly and Ganesha talking.

"So, what are your winter break plans?" Carmen asked Kelly.

"Actually, my family goes skiing every year, so we'll be going to our Tahoe cabin," Kelly said.

Wow. Bougie. No common ground there.

"I'll be spending winter break working and saving up as much as possible. But 'Nesha—" Carmen turned to her friend. "—any concerts?"

She, Ganesha, and Josie went to local punk rock concerts whenever they could find one playing in an all-ages venue. Ganesha led the charge most times, keeping track of her favorite musicians and where they were touring. Instead of Carmen's comment attracting Ganesha, Logan also became interested.

"Oh, what kind of music?" Logan said to the black-haired girl.

"Punk rock, I guess, or like, alternative?" she said. "There's this local band called The Jingle I like a lot. They've got a member who plays the French horn, and I love them."

Oh, SKA music, such a relic of the late '90s.

"I've heard of them!" Logan said enthusiastically. "I just started a band with those guys." Logan indicated Greg and Paul across the room with others from the water polo team.

"Oh yeah?" Ganesha asked. "What kind of music?"

"Rock and roll, babeeee." He pretended to riff a guitar, and Ganesha snorted. He returned to a normal tone of voice. "Actually, It's more bluegrassy than anything. I play the banjo."

"How cute!" Kelly giggled. "When you book your first gig, I'll be there." She touched his arm as she said this. The ugly green head of jealousy reared its head.

Interrupting their flirting, Carmen said to Kelly, "Oh, if you like punk, Kelly, Ganesha's pretty up on new music. Any recommendations for Kelly?" Carmen turned to Ganesha.

Ganesha narrowed her eyes at Carmen's odd behavior but directed her answer to Kelly. "Yeah, if you want, I can write down a couple."

"Cool," Kelly said, then turned back to Logan. "So, what's your band's name?"

Josie kicked Carmen in the shin, not very subtly.

Carmen's gaze shifted to the blonde, whose frown was palpable across the short distance. Okay, that had been a little heavy-handed. Cool it, Carmen.

"You guys want more?" Mattias discreetly held out the flask to Carmen and Josie. They both took quick swigs, making faces because of the taste. Mattias pulled Carmen out to dance, and she reluctantly followed, wanting to protest but not having a reason to. Carmen tried to drag Josie along, but she wasn't moving, having started a conversation with Ganesha.

Just as they got to the dance floor, Kelly and Logan joined them, along with Diego and his date. They danced for a while, and it was fun, but Carmen kept glancing over to Josie and Ganesha, who were still at the table. Mattias must have passed his flask to Josie because Carmen saw her take a swig after a furtive look around the room.

She didn't want to leave them out, so Carmen attempted to make her excuses to head back to the table after another song.

"Oh girl, you have to go to the bathroom? Me too!" Kelly snagged her arm before Carmen could protest. So, here they were, walking to the bathroom instead.

Carmen fished around for a way to say, '*Hey, I know you're here with Logan, but is there any way you've realized you're bisexual and might be interested in my friend Ganesha instead?*' There was no smooth or non-crazy way of saying any of that. Instead, Carmen gave generic platitudes about liking Kelly's dress, always a good conversation starter at a dance. "Did you and Logan plan on color-coordinating?"

"Yeah, I asked him to. Doesn't he look cute?"

Carmen thought he looked boring. Plain white button-up, black slacks, and black shoes. Nothing vintage, nothing colorful except for the red tie. He dressed nothing like her Logan. Not that clothes mattered. His personality was the same, no matter the haircut or clothes.

When they got to the bathroom, a couple of other girls were in there too, one of whom Carmen vaguely knew from Society, and Kelly knew from cheer. Kelly gushed to them while Carmen went into the stall before coming back out to wash her hands.

"Where are you applying for college?" Carmen said, for lack of anything else to say.

"I'm applying to a couple of schools, but I really hope to go to UCLA."

"What do you want to major in?"

"I honestly have no idea, but my older sister went to UCLA and loved it so..." Kelly shrugged.

Carmen didn't have the luxury of contemplating an Ivy League education with her first-generation parents, below-average grades, and no money. She'd also been depressed the first go-around through senior year — avoiding her parents, school, and responsibilities as often as possible. Community college had been her only option for continuing her education. But for Carmen, it had worked out well. She'd gotten her nursing assistant certificate first, then her Registered Nurse, without any debt. And she traveled once she had the money to, which was its own kind of mind-expanding life experience.

Carmen thought about how everyone hyped up the need to go to university, the closer to Ivy League, the better, regardless of the cost or any solid plan for post-graduation. Carmen remembered the conversation with twenty-seven-year-old Kelly at their high school reunion about the struggle to find a decent-paying job with a bachelor's and master's degree in philosophy. Adult Kelly had debated on getting a PhD to teach but was worried about the student debt she accumulated.

Carmen felt it had been so naive of her and so many of their classmates to want a university education without a plan. But she also compared adult Kelly with the teen Kelly that put powder on next to her. Adult Kelly seemed more complex somehow. She had openly flirted with Ganesha, and was the loudest, most out person in any room. A philosophy degree from UCLA may not have paid out in dividends, but it shaped reunion-Kelly into someone Carmen wanted to know.

Carmen reminded herself that teen and adult Kelly were the same person, they were just a decade apart in life experience.

Carmen thought on all this as she gave a sort of non-answer. "I've never been to UCLA."

"Oh girl, it's amazing. And my sister is in a sorority there, and the Greek life I heard is so much fun."

When Carmen and Kelly walked back into the gymnasium, Carmen begged off from going to the dance floor to "rest her feet" but really left to sit with her friends. They'd grabbed refreshments, and Josie offered hers when Carmen reached the table. When Carmen took a sip, she tasted a hint of Mattias's whiskey.

"So this is a school dance," Ganesha said in a deadpan tone. "I don't think we've been missing much."

"If you would come dance, it might improve your night." Josie took another sip of her whiskey-laced drink.

"I haven't heard a song worth dancing to yet," Ganesha said with a shrug.

Carmen's patience thinned. "It's fun dancing. You just need to loosen up a bit."

"I really don't want to drink, thanks." Ganesha frowned at them.

Defensively, Carmen muttered, "I didn't say anything

about alcohol."

"What else does 'loosen up' mean?"

"I just mean..." Carmen didn't know what she meant, except that adult Ganesha would not be sitting on the sidelines.

"I just mean, we're with good people. Kelly is really nice."

Her friend raised a well-formed black eyebrow at the non-sequitur. "Um, yeah, I guess."

"Kelly said you look nice in that dress." Which she had not. But Carmen felt that if Ganesha thought Kelly was interested, she'd show interest back.

Ganesha's frown grew wings. "I haven't said more than hello to her, and she's talking about my clothing?"

"And Kelly is really into politics. Maybe you guys could talk about that."

Josie's eyes widened, her expression screaming, 'Stop being weird, Carmen!'

Carmen, on a roll now, kept digging. "I just think she's nice, and you should give her a chance."

"A chance?"

"I mean, everyone is nice. You should give them a chance."

A song came on that Carmen knew Ganesha liked. "Look, you love this song. Come on." She dragged Ganesha onto the dance floor, Josie tailing them. Carmen led them to where Mattias and the rest danced in a loose circle. Carmen attempted to sandwich the Indian girl between her and Kelly. After an awkward bit of maneuvering, Kelly sidled up to Carmen instead. Ganesha was unintentionally squeezed out of the group and escaped back to the table with Josie.

A slow dance started, and Mattias held his hand

out to Carmen in mock gallantry. Carmen took it with reluctance. Was this sending signals she didn't want to send?

While they slowly turned in circles, Carmen couldn't help but watch Logan and Kelly dancing nearby. As if in slow motion, they drew closer and closer before Kelly turned her face up to his, and they kissed.

Carmen stiffened in horror, ignoring Mattias completely. She was shocked out of her brief stupor when a loud clatter caught her attention. She looked over the dancing couple's heads where a chair was tipped on its side. Next to it, Ganesha stood, fists clenched, hissing something at a still-seated Josie.

Pulling away from Mattias, Carmen made her excuses before rushing over to her friends. When she arrived, Ganesha whirled toward her.

"What is going on with you?"

"What?"

"Josie says you told her I'm... I'm..." Ganesha couldn't even say the word.

Josie slurred, "'Nesha was just wonderin' why you've been so weird. And you are being weird. You suck at subfer-subfu-subter—"

Carmen unhelpfully supplied, "subterfuge?"

"Yeah, lying. Tricking. You're just being weird, Ramen."

Ganesha looked ready to scream. Ignoring Josie's bumbling to get right in Carmen's face, she whisper-shouted, "Why are you telling people you think I'm gay?"

"I'm not telling *people*. I just told Josie that..." Carmen didn't know what to say.

"And *why* do you think I'd be interested in Kelly? Josie said you thought I might be interested in her. You didn't tell her too, right? I mean, I'm *not*...gay. I don't know what is wrong with you, Carmen, but you've been so weird lately. You've become this person... This person I don't even know."

Carmen flushed, stuttering her next words. "I-I-just-I just want you to be happy."

Ganesha's voice rose. "Do I look happy?"

"No, I just—come on, you can't pretend forever!" Carmen finally exploded. "I don't care who you're into, but you're letting your fear keep you from actually having fun! There's got to be more than just going to the movies and the park in this never-ending circuit! We do the same things, over, and over, and *over* again. It's *boring*."

Rearing back, Ganesha looked like Carmen had struck her. "Well, I had no idea we were getting in the way of all your *fun*. I didn't think it was such a *chore* to hang out with us. You don't have to. I'm leaving. I'll call my brother or something. Come on, Josie, let's go."

"Let me just explain." Carmen grabbed Ganesha's hand to stop her. "That all came out wrong. But come on 'Nesha, we're your friends. You can tell us if you're gay—"

A snigger came from the table near them. A few classmates watched their argument with amusement clear on their faces.

Ganesha went pale. Josie stood up, swayed, then threw up all over the floor at their feet. The entire room turned to look at them.

After Josie threw up, Ganesha rushed her out of the room, and Carmen was literally and figuratively left with the mess she created. She made vague "stomach-flu" excuses no one bought and felt obligated to help the janitor clean the mess. Disgruntled, he shooed her away.

Carmen remained for the rest of the dance if only so she didn't alienate Mattias too. She'd already been super weird tonight. She couldn't also ditch him halfway through the dance. There was an after-party at Diego's house, but with Carmen's mood after the explosive argument which led to her two best friends leaving, he dropped her off at home instead.

Before exiting the car, he took her hand and squeezed, sympathy on his face. "Hey, you don't have to tell me what happened, but I'm sorry. It looked like a bad fight."

With eyes tight and hot, she blinked rapidly a few times. "Yeah...I really messed up."

"I don't know you guys that well, but whatever it is, I'm sure you'll work it out. You've been friends with them forever, right? It'll be all right."

Josie and Ganesha were like family to her. Next to Logan, they were the most essential people in twenty-seven-year-old Carmen's life. In seventeen-year-old Carmen's life too. They'd gotten her through high school, through the roughest years of her life. They'd grown together.

Had they grown apart?

No. She was just expecting her best friends to act like their adult selves. But Ganesha was still a socially awkward teenager with raging hormones and little life experience. Carmen, at seventeen years old, had been just like her. Anxious and depressed and ready to get out of her teenage life and into the real world. Carmen benefited from the knowledge that everything turned out okay. Ganesha didn't know that. And Carmen was being incredibly unfair to her. Guilt and shame churned in her, hot and sour.

INTERMISSION

"The best thing for being sad," replied Merlin, beginning to puff and blow, "is to learn something."

The Once and Future King

CHAPTER 15

Unable to sleep, Carmen stayed up too late, her thoughts spiraling. She called and online messaged Josie and Ganesha when she got home, but neither responded. She stared up at the ceiling for hours, time stretching like taffy until she fell into a fitful doze in the early hours of the morning.

The next day, she called and messaged again, but their respective families said they were out, and their online avatars showed no activity on Instant Messenger. With a sinking feeling, she suspected they were blocking her. It was officially the start of winter break, so there would be no ambushing her friends before class. It would be easy if they wanted to avoid her for the next few weeks.

Carmen promised her parents she would pick up her lola—the Tagalog word for grandmother—from the airport that day. Around midday, sick of staring at unanswered messages, Carmen threw on fresh clothes and headed to the airport.

At the assigned baggage claim carousel, Carmen waited, eager to see her lola. The luggage belt started up and cardboard balikbayan boxes of all shapes and sizes turned around and around. She watched the escalators as the first wave of passengers came down and crowded around her. More and more people left, until there were only a few boxes and bags left. Carmen easily picked out her lola's things now that there were so few. She worried as the time ticked by. Maybe something had happened, and her lola missed her flight? Or Carmen had the wrong information and she'd shown up too early? Carmen had just decided to find the information booth when her lola came down the arrivals escalator, waving an arm in greeting.

Carmen hadn't seen her in person since grade school. Lola was still a handsome woman with wrinkled but soft velvety skin. She walked independently of any aids and regularly wore matching linen pantsuits and dress sandals with her short salt and pepper hair curled in at the ends.

In one of the few complete Tagalog phrases she knew, Carmen said haltingly, *"Pagpalain ka ng Dios lagi"* (May God bless you always). Remembering her manners, she touched the back of Lola's hand to her forehead. This, too, was a common respectful practice. Lola pulled her into a tight hug, smelling of tiger balm and baby powder. She pulled back and held Carmen by the shoulders, frowning at her.

"Hay nako, Apo. I waited at the gate forever for you!"

The gate? But Carmen always met people at the baggage claim. Security wouldn't let her...

Oh, wait. This was before 9/11. She could have just strolled right up to the gate. She winced, feeling bad for the mix-up.

"I'm so sorry, Lola. I thought this was where you wanted to meet," she said. "But look, I grabbed your bags for you!" Carmen gestured to the large, wheeled suitcase like it was a consolation prize.

Shaking her head, Lola offered a big smile and a squeeze. "Aye, I'm just glad not to have to take a taxi!"

Carmen insisted on taking the large suitcase and her purse as they made their way to her car. When they arrived, her lola exclaimed over the modest old beater.

"Aye, your own car! Look how big you are now! And so *guapa*." She received a pinched cheek with the last word, then a wink. "You must have a boyfriend?" All traditional grandmotherly things to say.

When they got home, her dad still lay asleep on the couch.

"Aye, your poor tatay, he has surgery tomorrow? I've been praying for him." Her lola crossed herself.

Many Filipinos were Catholic due to the heavy Spanish influence in the country. Lola was super Catholic. Like the kind of Catholic that goes to church every Wednesday and Sunday, wears a rosary wrapped around her wrist at all times, and talks about her priest like he's her best friend. Carmen's parents were more the 'go to church on Christmas and Easter' kind of Catholic. And again, since her dad's accident, not even then.

They did have a Santa Maria shrine, and it lit the front hallway red at night. It always gave her the creeps, the little woman doll-face glowing red like something out of a horror movie.

"Yeah, he's been in a lot of pain." Carmen looked down at his still sleeping face with concern.

"Aye, I'm glad to be here to help. Your nanay is so

worried about him."

Out of respect, Carmen only just stopped herself from a full eye roll. Her mom showed her concern poorly, constantly yelling and belittling him. They had fought just this morning before her mom left for work. There was still glittering glass in the kitchen corners from the cup her mom threw across the room.

Carmen helped Lola get settled in her room. She would vacate to the upstairs loft's pullout couch, as the condo only had two bedrooms. At least Carmen didn't have to be on the first floor with her parents. The downstairs echoed up to the loft, but with her grandmother visiting for the holidays and her dad recovering from his back surgery, there probably wouldn't be as many screaming fights in the living room.

Knowing she would have little privacy or access to her bedroom, Carmen dragged the desktop out to the loft and picked up extra shifts at the HollyJolly. Her estrangement from her best friends was an unexpected addition to Carmen's wealth of free time. It was going to be a long holiday.

The next day, solemn with trepidation, the family delivered her dad to the hospital for surgery. They waited in the lobby for a few hours, pacing, drinking over-sugared coffee out of Styrofoam cups, and snacking out of the vending machine. For once, Carmen and her mom didn't snap at each other when left together for too long. Carmen chalked it up to the addition of Carmen's level-headed lola being present.

After waiting an eternity in the cramped hospital chairs, a nurse wheeled her dad into a recovery room. He barely slurred together two words, groaning mostly. They left shortly after, and the next few days passed in a blur of hospital visits, working, and sitting around at home with her lola. Josie and Ganesha remained stubbornly silent, leaving all of her messages unanswered.

On one particular morning, she and her lola sat in the kitchen, listening to the radio and prepping a feast compared to what Carmen was used to. Carmen helped Lola cut vegetables for various pots boiling on every stove burner. In one, they boiled vermicelli noodles for pancit, some fragrant shrimp in coconut milk in another, and a fish head in stock in the third pot for sinigang soup.

"Lola, we can't possibly eat all this." Carmen protested but started rice on the last remaining burner. "The doctor isn't even sure if Dad is coming straight home or going to rehab tomorrow."

"Aye, all you had was frozen chicken nuggets and pizza. You need to eat, Anak. I'm here to feed you, your nanay, and tatay. *Ang kalusugan ay kayamanan.*"

Her lola was full of Filipino proverbs. This one roughly translated to '*health is wealth.*' Filipinos loved to eat. It was often how love was shown. A Filipino was more likely to ask you if you'd eaten — *Kumain ka na ba?* — than say hello.

When her dad worked in construction, many of his coworkers were Flipino. Back in those days, a crowd of construction workers often sat around their kitchen table after work, having a meal and a beer. More often than not with a coveted San Miguel or Red Horse, beers made in the Philippines. It wasn't even good beer, but it tasted like home to her dad and his friends.

After he was injured on the job and went on disability, their lives gradually changed. The friends stopped visiting, money became tight, and her mom earned the dubious title of "breadwinner." Her mom was never home to cook and her dad was in too much pain to try, so Carmen lived mostly off microwavables. Thus, Lola's obsessive desire to cook vast quantities of food in some vain attempt to make up for the lack of fruits and vegetables in their diet.

Without anyone else to talk to, Carmen spilled the sad story of the dance to her lola. Lola was a good listener too, and although she wasn't sure her lola could understand everything she said, she understood the gist.

"I really hurt Ganesha, and I don't have any excuses. I was totally in the wrong and just trying to pair off people for my own selfish reasons. But I should not have told Josie that Ganesha is gay. Even if it was just Josie, I know outing someone is a terrible thing to do. I just want Ganesha to be happy..." Carmen clenched her hands before she consciously loosened them, continuing her vegetable prep. "I know she can be so much happier than this. I feel like she and Josie are just stuck in like, like-high school." She knew she wasn't making any sense, so she tried to explain without saying, '*I traveled through time and Ganesha was happier out than in the closet.*' That wouldn't go over well.

"Like there's a whole wide world out there, and who cares what a bunch of high schoolers think about her, about any of us!" Lola squeezed her shoulder. Carmen, still trying to make her lola understand, continued to ramble. "I feel like I can see what our future is like, and it's *good*. Why shouldn't we get to live that life now?"

Her dark brown eyes, surrounded by the crow marks of a long life filled with both hardship and joy, looked pensive. "*Ang hindi lumingon sa pinanggalingan, hindi makakarating sa paroroonan.*" She laughed softly at

142

Carmen's look of confusion. "This is a proverb which means…a person cannot remember who they are without the journey. Does this make sense to you?" At Carmen's headshake, she continued. "You are only the experiences you've had. You cannot tell her how *you* would live her life. Maybe she will learn to be comfortable with herself, but she has to learn it in her own time."

For a long while after, Carmen thought about her words.

CHAPTER 16

Her mom came home in rare, good spirits that night, seeing Lola waiting in a kitchen full of good food. Over dinner, they talked mainly in Tagalog. Carmen couldn't understand a lot of it, but she enjoyed the ambiance. For a little while, at least.

Her lola, laughing at something her mom said, turned to Carmen and switched to English. "Apo, your nanay was so funny when she was your age. Nothing like you. She was always chasing after boys instead of focusing on school."

Her mom had a frown on her face now. "*Nanay*! Don't tell her these things."

"You gave me all my gray hair, Anak." She ran her fingers through her salt and pepper hair. "Your daughter should know the trouble you caused me."

"Carmen, don't listen to anything she says. I was a good girl. Yes, I was popular because I dress well and have a light complexion."

She did not need a color lesson from her mom. Filipino culture preferred lighter skin and could be prejudiced against darker skin. A whole host of skin-whitening products had been thrust on Carmen over the years.

Carmen's mom, sensing her daughter's annoyance, said, "I just think your skin would look better if you stayed out of the sun."

Her mom was forever telling her to 'get out of the sun!'

"Mom!" Carmen's voice took on a whining tone, pitched too high and shrill. "You're being such a racist."

"Aye! I'm not racist!" her mom yelled, then muttered the rest with a shake of her head. "So disrespectful, calling me names."

"I'm not calling you names, but you are prejudiced."

"If you just stayed out of the sun…"

"Mom, when have I been in the sun lately? It's winter!" Carmen hated this conversation. They had it all the time.

"It's all that running you do. Your skin is so dark it looks like you work in a field."

"Mom—"

"And I see you're finally wearing some of the clothes I bought you. See? I told you if you just tried the clothes I got you, you'd like them. Now, if you just wore some lipstick and did something with your hair…"

"Leave the hair alone." Carmen swatted her mom's hand away. "Maybe you shouldn't have married a dark-skinned, frizzy-haired man then!"

"Oh, always siding with your father." Her tone held notes of disgust. "You always loved him more than me. It's like I birthed his child and not mine. You are so thankless for everything I do for you, always defending your dad! He does nothing for you! *Walang hiya ka!*"

"I've got somewhere to be." Carmen stood, ready to be done with the conversation.

"Sit back down! I did not say you could go to your room." Her mom turned to Lola. "Aye, Nanay, she has no respect. These American children say whatever they want to their parents."

Carmen kept her tone deliberately calm, not wanting to get into a screaming match with her mom in front of her lola. "Mom, I actually do have to go. I have a closing shift."

"Fine, aye, go," her mom muttered with a wave of her hand, dismissive. Her mom turned to her lola, and they started a heated discussion in Tagalog, likely about Carmen.

Her dad got home the next day. Carmen was surprised the doctors decided he was safe to be home. He could barely get up to go to the restroom. He moaned the whole first day and needed obscene amounts of pain medication, which hardly seemed to touch his suffering. Her mom went to bed early, exhausted after caring for him hand and foot. Carmen stayed up with her lola making wire and paper mâché star lantern parols commonly used in the Philippines to celebrate Christmas processions.

Their family was from San Fernando, Pampanga, a province in the Central Luzon region of the Philippines. San Fernando held a lavish nine-day lantern festival for the holiday every year, thus claiming the title of "Christmas Capital of the Philippines."

Her lola shaped wire into the three-dimensional star shape. They were small as far as parols went, barely hand-sized. Carmen cut strips of thin multicolored paper and couldn't help but complain about her mom as they worked.

"I just don't understand why she's so mean all the time. She should have married a white guy if she wanted a white child."

"She loves you so much, Apo. can't you see that?"

"She has a poor way of showing it," Carmen muttered. She dipped each piece of brightly colored tissue paper in a mix of Elmer's glue and water and draped the metal-framed stars in them. Strung up with tiny lights, they would glow like stained glass. Carmen continued after a minute of concentrating on her handiwork. "And the way she treats Dad is just...it's terrible."

"She can be very bitter. I do not deny that. But, Apo, you have to understand that she has not had an easy life, and that can make a person...angry. Sad."

"Well, it's not easy for me or Dad either."

"You *have* had it easier just by being born in America. Your nanay, she had big dreams of going to college. But we were poor. She started working young to help take care of her younger siblings."

"I've been working since I was sixteen!"

"Yes, but only part-time, Apo. For spending money. And you have the option of college."

She had told her lola about her after-high school plans, about going to community college to become a certified nursing assistant, then a nurse. Or at least twenty-seven-year-old Carmen already did these things. Carmen sincerely hoped she got to go back to that life so she wouldn't have to repeat all that *school*. She told her lola about the other universities she was applying to. Even though Carmen hoped she wouldn't have to repeat the next ten years of her life, she might as well apply to some of the smaller state schools she'd applied to before, just to do it.

"Your nanay... she wanted that too. But it wasn't an option for us. She wanted so much more for herself than women in our province had. And...has she told you anything about...about her life before she came to America?"

Carmen shook her head.

"I don't know if I should tell you this." She looked toward the master bedroom to confirm the door was closed.

"What?" Her lola's look of guilt piqued her interest, and she leaned forward.

"I don't think she would like me telling you this, but it might help you understand her."

Her lola paused again, and micro-expressions flashed across her face as she debated something internally.

"I don't know if anything could make me understand her."

The resentment in Carmen's tone must have decided it for Lola, because she began talking. "You have to understand that she was the prettiest girl in the province. She had classic features and was very sought after."

She didn't need to hear more about how 'beautiful' her mom was. Carmen grimaced.

"One of our neighbors had a wealthy cousin who would visit their home, and your nanay caught his eye. She was dating someone else because she always was then, but he was persistent. And he was so kind to her and us. He'd shower her with gifts. He promised her everything. He proposed to your nanay, and she said yes."

"She was *married* before?" Carmen's voice carried louder than she intended.

Lola hushed her, eyes darting to the closed door again.

"Yes. They got married. And things seemed good for a while. She moved, and we didn't hear from her for a while. Then she told us she was pregnant."

"*What?*" Carmen whisper-shouted, totally forgetting to paper mâché until her lola urged her to restart.

Lola's lips pressed into a grim line. "The baby was stillborn. She had so much hope for that baby. She would write us these long letters about all her hopes and dreams."

Her lola shook her head, eyes cast downward. "They became pregnant soon after, and your nanay wasn't ready. She was fearful every day." Carmen braced herself again, dreading the answer. "She lost that baby too, in the womb. I don't know how many babies they lost."

Lola's wrinkled but still dexterous hands worked at the metal wire as she continued to speak. "She stopped talking about wanting children. She was so sad. She would lay in bed for days. Her husband...began to drink. And he turned out not to be such a kind man when he drank. He accused her of being cursed at one point and threw her out of the house in a drunken rage. It was the best thing he could ever have done for her. She came home."

With eyes wet and dull, she sniffed. "She was a different person when she came home. She had married very young, nineteen years old. Only a little older than you. But the four years she spent married to that man... and the losses! It took... She went to a hospital for people who have trouble...with their minds."

"An asylum?" Carmen said, shocked anew.

"For a little time, only a month," her lola rushed to say as if trying to reassure Carmen, but it didn't. "Before we

150

sent her, she wouldn't eat or talk, and she only slept. We had to get help for her. We sold all the jewelry that man had ever given her to get her treatment. But she came back better." Lola took a sip of tea before continuing.

"She met your father shortly after coming home from the hospital. They had only known each other maybe a few months when he asked her to marry him, and she said yes. He had just joined the U.S. Military and could get her to America, so she moved."

Carmen hadn't known this before but wasn't surprised. Her parents never fit well together. Even when her dad was healthy and able to support them financially, they hadn't gotten along. A short courtship was the least surprising part of this story.

"She became pregnant with you almost immediately. She didn't tell any of us back home until after you were born. She didn't even tell your tatay until she was getting big. Ask him. He will tell you that she denied being pregnant even to him. He doesn't know about…about everything else. He has no idea. But he told me once, years ago, how worried he had been that my daughter was nearly in labor before she would tell him she was pregnant, despite it being obvious."

This was a lot to digest.

"I just don't think your nanay ever recovered. She loves you…but she struggled after you were born too. She would call me, and I could hear you screaming in the background, and it sometimes seemed like…she forgot you were there… I don't know if she knew how to connect."

At Carmen's wide eyes, her lola rushed to reassure her. "I don't think you were ever in danger, or I would have told your tatay. She would tend to you, take care of your needs."

But Carmen knew she wasn't an especially touchy-feely parent. Never had been.

"And your tatay is a kind man, but I think…I think she only wanted to come to America. I don't know if she wanted everything…she has now."

Her lola was trying to put it kindly to her. Her mom hadn't signed up to be both breadwinner and caregiver to a daughter she always fought with and a disabled husband who—Carmen could admit—was addicted to pain medication. Which probably reminded her mom of her ex-husband's drinking problem now that she knew.

At least Dad is a non-violent addict, Carmen thought with a wince. She still struggled to think of her dad, who she loved with near hero-worship, as someone with an addiction problem. He was a functioning drug addict—well, as functional as someone with a back injury could be.

Carmen had never known any of this. She couldn't recall if she'd ever asked what her mom's life was like before she was born. It was the self-centered mind of the child to assume that their parents' lives started the day they were born. And she wasn't sure she wanted to know now that she had been told.

CHAPTER 17

After Lola went to bed, Carmen stayed up all night. She made dozens more parols. Once they dried, she hung them with Christmas lights so the whole living room glowed with the paper mâché stars.

At 5 a.m., she caught a rare smile and a wondrous look in her mom's eyes as she exited the bedroom, ready and dressed for work.

It was the least she could do for her mom by bringing a bit of Filipino Christmas magic into their home. She didn't know how else to reach out with all the bad blood between them. But Carmen had learned a lot the previous night, an ocean of silent history roiled under the surface of her mom's prickly exterior. Things weren't always as simple as, *"They're toxic. I don't need them in my life."* Sometimes it was about gratitude for the love they gave you, however much that love tasted bitter.

Winter break passed slow as molasses. She spent many

meals in the kitchen helping her lola cook and evenings sitting up late talking. Carmen dutifully helped her dad by helping him get up to go to the bathroom and driving him to his physical therapy sessions twice a week. They encouraged him to do his exercises at home despite his resistance to both the pain and the effort.

All through winter break Carmen drew, gaining confidence until finally, she opened up commissions on her journal. She could use the extra cash flow. She'd only ever traded art before, but she saw other artists on LyfeJournal charging small fees for commissions. Why couldn't she?

The TV was abuzz with Y2K fears and doomsday predictions of the entire computer network crashing, but Carmen knew it was nothing but talk. Her family stayed up on New Year's Eve, and Lola set up the Filipino New Year's altar. This practice mixed Filipino indigenous practices with Chinese superstition and Spanish Catholicism to make something uniquely Filipino.

They laid out bowls with round things, which signified prosperity—oranges and apples and grapes with a separate bowl for coins. There were twelve of each to symbolize bringing wealth into each month of the New Year. They made sticky rice to represent a strong family bond and pancit for its long noodles to symbolize a long healthy life. They stocked their water and rice dispensers so the New Year would overflow with prosperity. At midnight, they pulled loud poppers to drive away evil spirits. And even though Carmen was seventeen and nearly fully grown, her grandmother laughingly made her jump at midnight so she would "grow tall."

Before bed, just after midnight, she, her mom, and Lola scattered the coins throughout the house, in corners and between couch cushions, at the back of junk drawers, and even on the floors of their cars so they would "never be without money."

Even though her dad went to bed early due to pain and exhaustion, and her mom nagged at him, it was the best New Year they ever had. She could tell that her mom had mostly kept her tongue in check. Maybe because it was the start of a new year and the last year of the century. Or because it was bad luck to fight, or the lit parols scattered across the living room ceiling reminded her of her childhood. Regardless, Carmen noticed her mom's effort to keep the peace. It gave her a warm feeling in the pit of her stomach that she carried with her to bed, to the start of the New Year.

The last weekend of winter break, Lola answered the phone only to look towards Carmen with a curious tilt to her head. A moment later, she gestured to Carmen who sat drawing at the table.

"It's for you, Apo."

Setting her pen down, Carmen came to the phone. "Hello?"

"Hey, Trivia."

Carmen's eyes widened. Logan! She gave Lola a grin but tried to turn away from her curious gaze, keeping her tone flat and mild. "Hey, Logan."

"How is your holiday?"

"Really good, actually. Better than I thought it would be." Her lola gave her a thumbs up, then went into the living room to provide her with some privacy.

"That's great! Hey, so I'm calling because I've been memorizing lines all break, and I'm wondering if you'd want to run our scene for the play together?"

Time together during this wasteland of a holiday? *Yes.* Still in that flat, affected tone, she said, "Yeah, let's do it."

His tone was enthusiastic, puppy-like as always. "Perfect, you want to come over here tomorrow, say around 11 a.m.? We'll grab some lunch after?"

"Sure."

"Great."

Carmen's smile spread. "Great."

"Okay, bye…"

Logan had called her. Yes! When Carmen hung up the phone, her grandmother came back into the kitchen with a half-smile, her eyebrow raised in question.

"It's um. A guy from my theater club."

"Hmm? Just some guy?" Her tone dripped with sly humor.

"Yeah, just some guy." Carmen shrugged, feeling her cheeks redden. She refused to be a teenage girl about her feelings.

A hurried hour later, after having agonized in front of her closet before deciding to wear what she already had on, Carmen drove to Logan's. He answered the door wearing a pirate's hat and wielding a plastic sword.

"Aye, Tiger Lily? I didn't recognize yeh without yer costume."

She put her hands on her hips. "No notice was given that this would be a dress rehearsal!"

"Don't worry, I've got a canoe in the garage and some rope."

"Rope, huh?" Her eyebrows shot up to her hairline.

Logan winked before breaking character, laughing. "I'm not dragging you to our garage. Let's head upstairs. We'll go to the loft again."

Following him through the house, she covertly

looked at the decor. All the Christmas decorations were in white and silver, from the wreaths over the fireplace, the garlands around the banisters, to the baubles on the massive, flocked evergreen in the living room that stood nearly to the second floor. Nothing like the mismatched and homemade ornaments at home, with the dozens of multicolored parols hanging from the low ceiling in her dingy condo.

Still, she wouldn't trade her homemade ornaments for anything. After her parents divorced, she took their ornaments to save for herself. She was still using them ten years later. The one Christmas she and Logan spent together as twenty-six-year-olds, was celebrated at her apartment surrounded by her homely trimmings.

Upstairs, a snack platter was laid out, clearly by Logan's stepmom, although the house felt empty. Carmen didn't hear anyone, and there hadn't been any cars in the driveway. Carmen was grateful because she always felt so uncomfortable around his parents.

After some snacks and pleasantries, Logan dove in. "I really liked your Filipino native idea, and I want to use it for the play. I figured we could run our scene together a few times for practice, but it's a short scene. Once we're done, we can brainstorm how to get that sweet-sweet front-page credit. That would give my college application just the boost I need."

Her applications could also do with some flair. It was sparse on "achievements," considering the lackluster effort she had put into school before this year.

She and Logan ran their lines several times, with Carmen reading Tiger Lily and Peter Pan's lines and Logan reading both Hook and Smee's, which had them giggling into their manuscripts. They kept getting mixed up over who was reading which bits and would sometimes end up talking to themselves, in the case of Hook yelling at Smee.

After Logan and Carmen ran through the scene a few times, Carmen eventually lost her stiff self-conscious tone, and they moved on to changes they might make to the play.

"We've got to remove the 'Red Man' song and dance. Otherwise, changing it from Native American to Filipino natives would mostly be scenic. Palm trees and sand instead of forests and rivers. Grass skirts instead of leathers."

"Subtle. I like it!" He was nodding and taking notes.

"Yeah, we could remove the terrible stilted English."

"Okay, you're mentioning a lot to take out. How about adding stuff?"

She tapped her chin in thought, trying to think of what could be added. She thought of all the scenes which had the tribe in them.

"Hey, have you heard of Lapu-Lapu?"

He shook his head.

"He was the chief of the central region of the Philippines. You've heard of Ferdinand Magellan, right?"

"Like, the guy who went all the way around the world before America was discovered?"

"First, America was not discovered." Carmen held her finger up, all sass. "Hundreds of thousands of people already inhabited it."

"Right, right, right, okay. Got it." He gave a thumbs up. "So, like a long time ago."

"Yes, a long time ago," she said, with air quotes and sarcasm in her voice, before continuing in a lecturing sort of tone. "So, Ferdinand Magellan and Lapu-Lapu are a big deal in the Philippines. Everyone wants to say they're related to one or the other. Ferdinand Magellan was this sailor from Europe hired by this king to find an alternative spice route." Carmen wished she had a cell phone to look this up. She was somewhat vague on the specific details. "Spices were a big deal then — like struck-gold-rich. India was the source of most spices at the time. Europe already had spice trading routes going east or over land or whatever that brought them spices, but this was expensive. Europeans wanted a cheaper way to get spices. So they figured, hey, we've never gone west before. At this point, they knew the Earth was round, but they figured it couldn't be that far?"

"Can you teach my history class? I'm on the edge of my seat." He leaned in, eyes bright.

She could see the olive flecks in his irises this close. She leaned back, self-conscious, and frowned at him. "Do you want to hear this, or do you want to make fun of me?"

"I'm not! Seriously, Trivia, this is fascinating. Go on." He held his hands up in apology.

"Okay, so Magellan and a bunch of other boats go south through the Atlantic Ocean to Patagonia. Despite losing like half their boats to starvation and mutiny, they make it across a body of water called "the peaceful sea," which we call the Pacific. Pacify, get it?"

"Mind. Blown. Go on..."

His enthusiasm seemed genuine, so she continued."There are over 7,000 islands in the Philippines, and they just so happened to touch down in nearly the center, where there was already this ongoing feud between two chiefs of neighboring islands. Magellan's fleet at this point is only down to like two to three big ships, from like five. So they send in a few people to shore to make a deal with the chief of Cebu for food, housing, and directions. This Chief, called Don Carlos, I think? He was the chief of Cebu and made a deal with the Portuguese. He saw the fancy guns they had and the armor, and he thought, 'why don't I send these guys against my enemy?' So Don Carlos says, 'Magellan et al. Kill Lapu-Lapu and defeat the Mactan tribe, and I'll let you make landfall, feed your people, and tell you where to go from here.'"

"Shady business!" Logan whistled.

"Right? I mean, it sounded like a good plan. And the Portuguese thought, 'these natives don't know what will hit them.' So they agreed."

Knowing how to use a suitable pause in a story when she needed one, Carmen took another sip of water. "So, the next morning, Magellan and his men storm the coast of the island of Mactan. But they lose—*bad*. Despite heavier artillery against the local people carrying handheld weapons. Magellan doesn't even make it to shore! Despite history painting him as this globe-circling superhero, he died on the shores of the Philippines. And the Mactan Chief Lapu-Lapu? The way my family always liked to tell it was that Lapu-Lapu cut off the head of Magellan and put it on a spike facing the remains of his crew still on the boat."

After pausing again for dramatic effect, Carmen said, "And the rest of his body? They *ate for dinner*." Carmen emphasized the last line, and Logan gasped.

Logan's expression looked like he was digesting the story, while Carmen grinned like the cat that caught the canary.

"Okay, first, that was so gruesome. Second, I love it. Back at it again with the facts, Trivia! Lapu-Lapu is my hero."

"I know, right?"

"Let's see if we can sneak this guy into our play. I don't know if the chief has many speaking lines or is named, but *we'll* know who he is. Did Lapu-Lapu have a daughter? Can we use her name for your character?"

"Not that I know of...but I've been thinking. There's a traditional Filipino name. It's actually my grandmother's name. Luwalhati. Tiger Lily. It's even the same number of syllables! It means Glory."

"I love it! Let's iron out some details and pitch this idea to Mrs. Malone. We are getting those credits *for sure!*"

ACT TWO

"Time flies like an arrow, fruit
flies like a banana."
Groucho Marx

CHAPTER 18

The last week of winter break passed in a blur. Carmen and Logan met twice more, and she basked in his attention. That was until, in casual conversation, she realized Logan and Kelly were still hanging out, likely *romantically*. That shut down any potential hope in her about anything happening between them.

Lola flew back home on the last day of winter break. Carmen dreaded this parting, knowing it would be a genuine and final goodbye. In just a few short years, her lola would die in her sleep. It had been quick and painless, and she'd been active until nearly the day before. Her lola was elderly. It wasn't a thing to prevent. But Carmen didn't want to let her go.

When twenty-one-year-old Carmen heard of her lola's passing, she'd only been sad in the way that distant relatives passing would make a person unhappy. But Carmen knew her grandmother now. Her lola had helped her understand her family so much more in those few short weeks. She had shown her kindness and sympathy while Carmen struggled with being estranged from her friends and her constant fights with her mom. They'd grown close.

Staying up late to chat with Lola, she tried to memorize every story, every nuance, every axiom. She desperately wished video chat was more prevalent. She tried to figure out if Skype had been invented yet—it hadn't. Instead, she set her lola up with an email despite not owning a computer. Lola promised she would find a younger neighbor or grandchild to help her set something up. She pledged to call too, not just to her mom but specifically to talk to Carmen.

Her composure didn't break until she gave her one final hug. Watching her lola walk onto the jet bridge, and out of sight, made the dam break. The flood of tears came, and she wept bitterly. She locked herself in an airport bathroom and allowed herself a total breakdown, nearly hyperventilating with tears. She hated being alone right then, but there was no one to confide in and no way to explain why she was so desperately sad. She eventually gathered her wits and went home, a hollow pit in her chest.

Her best friends didn't answer a single one of her emails, AIM messages, or phone calls by the end of winter break.

A twinge of hope sparked in her when she spotted Josie in their economics class on the first day of school. She sat right behind the blonde and tapped her shoulder. Josie swiveled in her chair and her eyes widened in recognition. Then she frowned and faced forward again, her shoulders hunched.

Taking a deep breath, Carmen hoped her apology would be enough. Josie hadn't said a word to her yet, so

Carmen dove in headfirst, trying to get in what she had to say while Josie was stuck with her.

"I put you in a terrible spot, and I shouldn't have said *anything* to you about 'Nesha. It was a stupid plan, trying to set everyone up, and I'm sorry."

Sighing, Josie turned back slowly. "Yeah, I mean...I also played a role in how everything went down with Ganesha. But you said some terrible things."

"I don't think you guys are boring," Carmen rushed to say. "I don't know what I was saying. I love you guys! You and Ganesha are my best friends in the whole world. You're more like family to me than anything."

Josie still frowned at her. "It hasn't felt that way. You've made a lot of new friends this year, and that's fine, but it doesn't feel like you've wanted to be our friends too. You've been acting like you've had better things to do than hang out with us."

Her hand came up when Carmen tried to interrupt. "And I guess it's not terrible, you telling me you think—" Josie whispered this part, leaning forward. "—'Nesha might be gay. But you were being obvious and pushy at the dance."

She wanted to interrupt, to apologize again, but Josie kept talking.

"And those classmates in our Model UN overheard you. They've started *teasing* her so now 'Nesha wants to quit so she doesn't have to see them again."

Wrenching guilt opened a pit in her stomach, almost nauseating in its intensity. Before she could keep babbling apologies, the bell rang, and their teacher called attention to the front of the room. Carmen couldn't recall a thing from the lesson as she stared at Josie's blonde ponytail from behind. She didn't know how to fix this, but she desperately wanted to.

After class, Josie turned to her, looking firm and not very sympathetic to Carmen's attempts. "Hey, so 'Nesha... She is still really pissed at you. It, uh, may be a good idea to eat lunch elsewhere for a while. Let her cool down about the whole thing."

"I don't know how to fix this, but I am *really, truly* so sorry. If she'd just...*talk* to me, maybe I could convince her."

Josie's voice softened at what must have shown on her face. "Listen, I'll work on convincing her to accept your apology. But Carmen—" Josie suddenly looked severe as they exited the classroom. "—you *outed* her. You had no right, and...I gotta make sure Ganesha knows this doesn't... She isn't going to lose both of us as friends."

Carmen was left in the crowded hallway, feeling bereft. She cursed ever being sent into the past. She cursed herself and her big fat mouth. She wished she could undo all of it. Why couldn't she go back in time now when her whole life felt turned upside down and... *wrong*. Erase the entire dance and get a do-over.

She was already miserable when she found herself ten years in the past, a time in her life when she had so little—no autonomy, no money, and no Logan. But at least she could count on having Ganesha and Josie. But she messed it all up by being a thoughtless *jerk*.

Why was she *here* and *now* instead of back in her comfortable, happy, uncomplicated, guiltless twenty-seven-year-old life? She resolved to make contact with Mrs. Malone's daughter somehow. Maybe she was the key to getting back to her time.

On the first night of Society, Carmen arrived early to try for a more casual conversation with Mrs. Malone.

Only a few people were in the auditorium early, most having gone home to eat dinner before coming back for rehearsal. Mrs. Malone stood at the center of the room with a ruler and masking tape. Carmen offered to help her divide the room and lay tape lines where audience chairs would be set up. They worked quietly for a minute, Carmen trying to figure out how to bring up her daughter casually.

"So, Mrs. Malone, what did you do during winter break?"

"Nothing special. I rarely leave town on holidays."

"Oh! Do you have family here in town? Children?"

"Yes, I have one daughter." Mrs. Malone bent to reposition a piece of tape she laid crooked.

"How old is she?"

"She's in grade school. Here, you've measured that short, I can tell. The rows are supposed to be two and a half feet wide, not two feet."

Carmen tried again. "You look too young to have a child in grade school!"

Mrs. Malone's eyes narrowed. "No, I don't. I had her at forty-two, practically menopausal. Are you flattering me for a reason? Do you want to play the lead in the next play? Because flattery won't get you the role of Dorothy." Her teacher flashed her a half-smile.

A lightbulb of an idea flickered in Carmen's mind. "Actually, I babysit. I'm trying to save up some money, so I'm always looking for new families to babysit for." Carmen knew she rambled, but fibs always led to oversharing. She hadn't babysat a day in her life unless nursing counted. Which Carmen thought it did. Adults in the hospital were just like cranky children.

"Oh, you wouldn't be able to babysit Alice. She has

several medical conditions, so we don't like to leave her with strangers."

Alice! She finally had a name to go with the mystery girl.

"I'm certified in CPR, if that helps. And I've been helping care for my dad, who had surgery this last winter break." Twenty-seven-year-old Carmen was more than certified in CPR. She was a nurse with critical care experience.

"She has cerebral palsy, a seizure disorder, and is deaf, so you wouldn't be able to talk to her either."

"I'm fluent in American Sign Language."

"You are?" She stopped taping to look up at Carmen in surprise.

Nodding, Carmen continued in sign language. "And even if she has a seizure while I babysit her, I know what to do. Prevent her from injuring herself, time the seizure, and call 911 if the seizure lasts too long."

Now Mrs. Malone looked properly surprised.

"Oh." She continued, still in sign language. "And I won't put anything in her mouth. People used to think seizing might cause someone to swallow their tongue, so they would stick a tongue depressor in their mouth, but that's stupid." Carmen remembered the high school reunion event that somehow led her to be in the past. "And I know the Heimlich."

By this point, Mrs. Malone's eyebrows were in the vicinity of her hairline.

"Well, if the perfect babysitter falls into your lap, you say yes." She shook her head, half-talking to herself. "Thank you, Carmen. We'd love that. My husband and I haven't had a date night in years." Her teacher looked pensive. "You know, it's weird actually..." She paused in thought.

"What is?"

"Alice kept asking me about the club and wanting to come, even though it would be boring for her, watching us rehearse lines and paint backdrops. Anyway, she kept asking about the people in the play. I think now she was asking about you. She kept asking about a curly-haired student I have."

Feigning bewilderment, Carmen said, "Hmmm, no idea. Anyway, let me know when and where, and I'll be there." It was good that Alice had asked after her because it further proved they knew each other previously. Maybe if they both traveled through time, they could somehow figure out how to get back together.

Mrs. Malone started taping again. "I'll have to talk to my husband, but we can work something out soon."

"Thanks, Mrs. Malone."

Finally! Carmen had a name, a possible way to spend time with Alice, and further proof that they might know each other from the future.

In the following weeks, Carmen worked as many hours at the HollyJolly as she could. With her best friends scarce, weekends were social deserts.

Logan and Carmen successfully pitched their modifications to the play. There were other good ideas, but everyone loved their changes best by consensus. Since her role as Tiger Lily, now Luwalhati, was only one scene of the play, Carmen joined the prop and scene-making group again. The props were all made to be island-themed instead, which fit in nicely with the whole mermaid and pirate plot. It was a subtle but exciting transformation.

The courtyard was ground zero for awkward social interactions at lunchtime, as everyone gathered with their friends, with nowhere for Carmen to sit. So she avoided it like the plague. Logan, Kelly, and Mattias were the only other students at school Carmen knew enough to greet in the halls, but not well enough to join their respective lunchtime seating arrangements.

Instead, Carmen took her midday break in her parked car. Josie had told her to wait for Ganesha to come to her, and she was trying to honor that, as lonely as it was.

She'd forgotten how much high school sucked. She was aware of the cliques and the high school social networks she wasn't a part of, but as long as Carmen had her best friends, it hadn't bothered her that she was *different* from many of her classmates. This was ritzy Southern California. In a sea of Mustangs and BMWs and Hummers, she drove a nearly twelve-year-old Ford Escort in chipped, bland, unfashionable beige. She felt insignificant. And lonely.

Winter gradually bled into spring like one long gray nightmare. Maybe nightmare was too strong a word. But she was heartsick and homesick for her old life and miserable without the steady presence of Josie, Ganesha, or Logan.

CHAPTER
19

While each day seemed to pass agonizingly slow, Carmen was surprised to find that spring break was a short two weeks away. Dress rehearsals started that week for *Peter Pan*, and students were abuzz with talk of their week-long holiday plans.

Ganesha hadn't spoken a word to her since the dance and had needed space. Carmen gave it to her, but she feared 'Nesha would never forgive her. But just as the cold weather thawed, so too did Josie's demeanor toward her. They chatted before and after their one shared class, although they still hadn't spent any time together outside of economics.

"So, the Model UN is doing this trip to UC Berkeley for the California State Conference." Josie twisted around in her seat to look properly at Carmen seated next to her. "I convinced Ganesha to rejoin for her college apps, so she's going too. We've both been waitlisted for UC Berkeley. The conference is only a day, so we decided to turn it into a road trip and visit some schools. Do you, uh... Do you have any plans for spring break? Want to come?"

Hope fluttered in her chest at the offer. "I mean, will Ganesha..."

"Start eating lunch with us again and just...just keep being yourself. Remind her of why she was friends with you in the first place."

Carmen hated the past tense of their friendship.

"I just..." Josie said. "There are only like two and a half months of high school left, and you guys have been my best friends forever. I can't imagine making this trip without you."

When Carmen lived this year the first time, she hadn't had the funds or the desire to go on Josie and Ganesha's big college trip. She also hadn't been fighting with them either, so there hadn't been the desperate need to spend time with them. She took this as the olive branch it was. "I would love to." Carmen smiled wide, despite her trepidation.

Stepping into theater class, Carmen expected to see Kelly and Logan's usual flirtatious behavior. She'd endured watching them hold hands, flirt, pass notes, and generally gravitate toward one another for the last few months, leaving little room for others. However, when she seated herself, she noticed a definite chill between the couple as they sat on opposite ends of the room, studiously avoiding each other. She felt guilty, like a bad friend to them both, for hoping they had broken up.

That evening at dress rehearsal, Carmen asked Logan to help her move some props under the pretense of talking to him.

"Hey, you okay?" she asked as they moved a large

scene piece.

"Yeah...Kelly and I broke up, and I'm still pissed about the whole thing."

"I'm sorry, that sucks." I hoped it sounded like a generic, totally not awkward answer.

"Yeah." Logan was quiet for a minute as if debating what to share. "It wasn't even over anything big." The words burst out of him as if he tried to hold back but needed to vent to someone. "I mean, we've only been dating a few months, but she wants me to rearrange my whole life for her, which is ridiculous!"

Carmen made sympathetic noises. Logan continued in an apparent non sequitur. "I got an early acceptance to UC San Francisco for their music program."

"That is awesome!"

"Yeah, I'm psyched about it. My dad isn't happy because he still wants me to join the Marines like him. And according to him, music is for pansies." Logan said this last part with a mocking tone, his face twisted up. "He's such a douche."

Though Carmen secretly agreed, she couldn't say it aloud.

"I'm sorry, Trivia," Logan said, interrupting his own story to apologize. "You only asked how I am. Things suck."

"No, it's okay. Get it off your chest. So...you and Kelly?"

"Right, so she got into UCLA and tried to convince me to go instead. I got into both schools, but UC San Francisco was always my dream program. My dad wants me to go to UCLA too, because he doesn't want me to pursue music. It was just frustrating, my girlfriend siding with my dad about my future. I mean...we've only been dating a few months! There was other stuff, but...I shouldn't be unloading all of this on you. It isn't right. I'm sorry."

"It's okay." Carmen shifted her shoulders downward in discomfort. She'd asked but was regretting it now.

"So..." he said, clearly wanting to change the subject. "Are you doing anything fun for spring break?"

"My friends invited me to tour schools in the Bay Area."

"Hey!" He brightened at this. "I'll be in the Bay Area for spring break too! I've got an extra ticket to Mamma Mia now, that new play with all the ABBA songs. Anyway, if you make it to San Francisco, let me know. It would be really fun!"

"Yeah!" Realizing that she had a lot of making up to do with her friends, she hesitated. "But...I've got to clear it with Josie and Ganesha. I don't want to get into the details, but I made a huge mistake and am trying to make it up to them."

"I can probably get them tickets too." He shrugged. "The more, the merrier! My dad knows someone who knows someone, I guess."

"That would be awesome!"

A girl Carmen didn't know well, but whom Carmen had seen with Kelly in the hallways before, all dressed in their cheerleader uniforms, leaned over into Logan's space.

"I see we've moved on already, huh?"

Her eyes followed them as she moved past to the supplies closet.

"I'm sorry, Jessie's never really liked me." Logan's face burned with embarrassment. "She's Kelly's friend and...Kelly's upset, so..." He shrugged again.

Carmen couldn't believe she was saying this after working so hard at trying to catch Logan's attention, but she had her self-respect to think about too. "This is just as friends, yeah? I mean, you just got out of a relationship —"

"Yeah, of course!" They both had color in their cheeks now, and she cursed herself for saying it. "I mean, you're cool, Trivia. I wouldn't rebound like that. That wouldn't be right."

"Thanks." His eye contact lingered, and she broke it, looking down and away.

He had a flirty lilt again to his voice. "And you'll know if I'm asking you out."

She kept her eyes firmly away, and their conversation grew superficial as they continued moving equipment.

After being coached many times by Josie on what not to say during lunch, Carmen finally joined her and Ganesha again. Josie said not to apologize or acknowledge the whole fiasco at the dance in no uncertain terms. Ganesha didn't even want to talk about it with Josie. She tried to ignore that it ever occurred.

At lunch, Ganesha wasn't hostile toward Carmen. She just avoided talking directly to her at any point. Carmen would say something, Josie would respond to her, and Ganesha would react to what Josie said. Most people wouldn't even notice, but this wasn't their usual dynamic. Carmen and Ganesha were the talkers, with the occasional zinger by Josie. Poor Josie had to make double the conversation as the go-between for her feuding friends.

"I'm looking forward to the trip. What day is your conference?" Carmen directed the question to both of them, but Ganesha just stared down at her food.

"It's Friday," Josie said eating her sandwich slowly, picking it apart, "so I figure we'll drive up Wednesday, check out UC Santa Barbara on the way, then go past Berkeley to Davis Thursday. The conference is only a couple of hours later in the day Friday, so we can check out Berkeley then."

Ganesha spoke mainly to Josie. "I'd like to go to San Francisco for just a day to sightsee Saturday, then early Sunday we can drive home."

Enthusiastic, Carmen directed her response to Ganesha. "I love that idea. There are a few places that would be fun to go to."

Ganesha didn't acknowledge or reply and untucked a curtain of her shiny black hair to block her view of Carmen.

"Oh yeah?" Josie said.

Carmen's gaze lingered on the curtain of black hair separating her from Ganesha before turning to Josie. "Yeah, let's go to the bridge and Chinatown for some food, and there's a pretty cool beatnik coffee shop and bookstore in North Beach we should check out."

Josie, with perhaps more enthusiasm than was warranted, said, "Awesome! You've done your research!"

She hadn't done any research, but twenty-seven-year-old Carmen lived there.

Filling the weird gaps in the conversation where Ganesha would usually have chimed in, Josie said, "Let's do it. 'Nesha, is there anywhere specific you were thinking of going while in San Francisco?"

"I'd like to see the wharf and a play if possible. They've got a bunch of Broadway shows going this spring, but they're expensive."

Carmen tentatively responded, worried that bringing

up Logan, whom Ganesha associated with the dance, might trigger her anger. "I may be able to get us free tickets to Mamma Mia?"

Again, Josie spoke up after another beat, where Ganesha would normally respond in the past. "Free sounds great!"

"Yeah, um...Logan told me he's planning on visiting UC San Francisco during spring break, and his dad has some hookup and may be able to get us free tickets?" Everything she said sounded like a giant anxious question mark.

Ganesha grunted.

"That would be awesome," Josie said. "We're already tight on cash this trip as it is. Make sure to bring extra pillows because we may have to sleep in the car at some point. We may even want to scrounge up a tent somewhere. Beach camping is cheap, right?"

Carmen realized she was short on a few essential details. "Which car should we take? Jo', your car is tiny and would be hell to sleep in, and I'm not sure it's road-trip worthy. My car is even smaller than yours."

The blonde paused to let Ganesha answer, but when she didn't, Josie spoke. "Ganesha is going to borrow her brother's minivan." Ganesha's oldest sibling was almost thirty and was the only sibling not living in the home any longer. He had a wife and daughter, with another on the way. They had a family van Ganesha occasionally borrowed.

"*Way* more comfortable. Cool, I think my dad has an old tent in the attic somewhere from when he tried to get us to go camping years ago. I'll ask him when I get home."

Again, they both turned to Ganesha, who remained

stubbornly quiet.

Half to herself, Josie mumbled, "Sounds like we've got a plan."

This trip was going to be...interesting.

CHAPTER
20

Peter Pan **played to** a packed house all three nights, and their audience gave them rave reviews. Not that there was any sort of competition for good or bad high school productions, but audience engagement was apparent, with rounds of applause at multiple points in the play. Lapu-Lapu the chief was cast last minute, and although he had no lines, his bloodthirsty appearance—with a head on a spike—gained 'oohs' and 'aahs' from the crowd.

They fashioned a Filipino traditional double outrigger boat, called a Bangka, for Luwalhati to be tied up in by Hook instead of the canoe in the original. She even wore traditional Filipino indigenous clothing, lots of woven red and white and black fabric, and a beaded headband. Carmen's grandmother mailed the dress from the Philippines, with the only caveat being that Carmen send a picture of her in full regalia on stage in the Bangka. When Carmen told her about the name change from Tiger Lily to her grandmother's first name, she could hear the emotion in her lola's voice, happy to be included in some way.

With flair, Logan pulled off the Hook role. He played it more like Jack Sparrow and less British than the Disney version. He glued on bushy black eyebrows that he skillfully waggled as he swash buckled across the stage. He stole the show from Peter Pan, who was played by a girl who had that high school theater way of overacting every line.

Carmen's parents attended the final night. She saw them seat themselves from her spot in the stage wing, her dad still struggling to navigate with a cane. Carmen also spotted Alice just before the lights dimmed. Mrs. Malone had made vague promises about needing a babysitter at some point, but no concrete plans had been made. Carmen needed to find some way of signing for Alice to wait after the production so they could talk.

She played her part one last time, tied up in the boat, delivering her lines with all the skills she had, which were few. She at least said them correctly, if not memorably. Hook, Smee, and Peter's antics had the audience rolling with laughter. Peter whisked her down the center aisle and through the back doors. Breathless and laughing, they looped around to the stage door, and then she was backstage again, with everyone rushing around, getting in and out of costume and props being moved from one side to the other. Before she knew it, they were bowing once again, the last performance over.

When she took her bow, she looked directly at Alice, subtly giving the sign for *wait*, which was done with both hands, palm facing up and fingers spread out. It was subtle, and she could do the sign with her arms linked with the other actors during their bow. But the movement and the eye contact were unmistakable to Alice, who nodded.

Carmen, who didn't have as much of a role backstage in this play, went to talk with Alice and her dad as soon as she was free to do so.

"Hi, Mr. Malone? I'm Carmen. Did your wife tell you about me? I wanted to meet you and Alice." Carmen signed as she spoke aloud.

"Yes! She said you might be available to babysit. Meet Alice." Easily, six foot plus, Mr. Malone towered over her. A reed of a man with an impish grin.

Carmen's parents, seeing her, came over and struck up a conversation with Mr. Malone, giving her and Alice some semblance of privacy in that at least Mr. Malone wasn't looking directly at them.

Still, for appearances, she introduced herself. Alice did the same, signing her name by spelling it, then giving her sign name, an 'A' spinning a wheel.

"You know, because of the wheelchair," Alice said. "Even at my school for the deaf, there aren't very many kids in wheelchairs." Alice wore skin-tight gloves for her wheelchair wheels, so when she pushed herself she wouldn't get her hands dirty.

"That..." Carmen signed, distracted by the introduction. "Isn't that offensive? Like, are they making fun of you?"

"No! I love my wheelchair. Without it, I would have no way of getting around." She patted a wheel with a gloved hand. "I still sometimes practice with braces, but my wheelchair gets me where I need to go."

Remembering she had more pressing matters than nicknames to discuss, Carmen shook her head. "Have we met before? You signed my sign name at the previous play."

"Yes...this may sound crazy..."

"I promise you, it won't. Because I've met you before," Carmen signed.

"I met you in a dream. And...I feel so crazy for saying this. But I'm not seven...and I've somehow been..."

Carmen could tell it was too weird even to sign, so Carmen finally came right out with it. "Did we both travel in time? I was twenty-seven one day and seventeen the next. Do you remember the reunion?"

Alice nodded fervently, looking relieved to have this confirmed, that they weren't both just crazy for remembering a whole decade of life no one else had experienced.

Before they could say more, Mrs. Malone approached, and they had to change topics mid-sign.

Alice signed, "I'm learning a lot in school right now about reading."

"Carmen! I see you found my family!" Mrs. Malone smiled at them both. "Yes, Alice is quite gifted. I don't know how she's advanced so much this year, but I've found her reading chapter books! Quite long ones! And she's so young!" Alice rolled her eyes at Carmen, but only so her mom couldn't see. When Mrs. Malone looked back at her daughter, she smiled brightly, no trace of the teenage eye roll present.

"Carmen is fun! I'm looking forward to her babysitting me."

Carmen's mom and dad shifted their attention from Mr. Malone to their conversation.

"I had no idea you knew so much sign language Carmen," Carmen's dad said. "I'm proud of you! And you were so good in the play. Wonderful production you put together, Mrs. Malone. My daughter has loved being in the drama club."

Her dad could always be counted on to gush about her.

While they chatted, her dad leaned heavily on his cane. By the time Mr. and Mrs. Malone expressed the need to head home, her dad's knuckles had turned white and shook with the effort. They said their goodbyes, and Carmen walked out with her parents, letting her dad hang off her arm as they left. She had driven herself to the play, so they parted ways in the parking lot with the plan to meet at home for dinner.

When Carmen walked up the path to their condo, her dad sat on the ground just inside the flung-open front door, her mom looming over him.

"Carmen, do you see this?" Her mom jabbed a finger toward her dad. "*Susmaryosep*, Manuel, aren't you embarrassed to have your daughter see you this way?"

"I just slipped. It's fine."

"Oh God, are you okay?" Carmen rushed up the porch steps to help him. His cane had slid halfway down the hallway, so she used her body to leverage him up.

Carmen's mom answered before he could. "He's fine, just high!"

"I'm not high. My cane just slipped."

His hands trembled as Carmen handed him his cane. He laboriously shuffled down the hallway and her mom berated him as he lowered himself into a chair with a groan.

"He popped two pills in the car on the way home. Manuel, you couldn't even wait an hour to take your pills? Do you store them in all your pockets? I swear, I will find you dead one morning, and I just can't live this way!"

"It's fine! I take them when I'm supposed to!" Carmen's dad said firmly. Then his voice softened as he directed his following words to Carmen. "I just wasn't watching where I was walking, honey."

"Carmen, do you see him? He's an addict who can't even go three hours without his fix!"

"Flor! Stop it! The medication hasn't even kicked in. I'm just in pain!"

"I will not stop it. Your daughter needs to know what you are, an addict! I counted your pills. You don't think I know how much more you take than you should? This is not how anyone should live! You're just wasting your life away, and mine too..."

Carmen escaped to her room, shutting the door firmly behind her. She put a CD in her Walkman and put her headphones on at full volume to drown out the noise as she packed. She wouldn't be leaving for another two days. But since she had taken a bunch of shifts at the HollyJolly to make up for her spring break expenses, she wouldn't have much time to pack.

When she got home from work the following Monday night, she found a big fat envelope from San Jose State University in the mailbox. Knowing what a big envelope meant, she rushed to rip it open and zeroed in on the word, 'Congratulations.' She backtracked and read slower, not believing her eyes. Not only had she gotten accepted to San Jose, but they were offering her a scholarship to go. It wouldn't cover the total cost, but there was still time to save and apply for more scholarships. Carmen felt a warm flush of pleasure at this development.

When she lived through this year the first time, she hadn't made it into any of the schools she applied to, forcing her to go to community college. It had been a blessing in disguise because she couldn't have afforded it anyway and hadn't known how to navigate the confusing financial system to find scholarships.

Carmen was older and hopefully a little wiser now. She knew she would go for nursing again if she had to live the next ten years over. But...getting to go to a university without falling into debt would be amazing. It was something she always thought she missed out on, the traditional college experience—dorms and cafeterias and school pride. Community college had given her the training she needed, but there wasn't that quintessential college lifestyle her friends talked fondly of.

She would let her friends know when they picked her up early the following day about her acceptance, and maybe they could work San Jose into their trip. What was the mascot for San Jose? Perhaps she'd get a sweater, or a T-shirt, maybe ask if they had tours for incoming students. Carmen wanted to tell her parents, but it was late, and the house was dark. They were likely asleep. Too excited not to share the news with someone, she got on her LyfeJournal to write a journal entry.

> "I got into one of the schools I applied to! And they offered free money for me to go! Like money I don't have to give back! Scholarships are a fantastic invention—free money to students. Why do they exist? Where does the money come from? Why are they just giving it to me and all I have to do is go to school, which is what I want to do anyway? It's not really a win-win. I feel like I'm the only

one winning. Well, and the school, because they get obscene amounts of money.

"I haven't gotten to tell my parents yet. I don't know if they'll be proud or just relieved to be rid of me. I'm pretty sure my mom hates us all and can't wait for me to be out of her life and be one less burden she has to put up with. She and my dad had a beast of a fight a couple of days ago, and I'm not surprised by it anymore. I just walked out and carried on with my day. Just an average day in this household. But soon, I won't have to put up with it anymore because I'm off to college and out of this mess!"

Her alarm went off too early the following day, and Carmen got ready and out the door in record time. The sky was a dark predawn deep blue, stars still visible but fading fast. The air felt light and crisp and full of potential. Or maybe it was just her excitement for the trip and the acceptance letter giving her poetic feelings.

Sipping her coffee, Carmen waited on the curb. When her friends arrived, she piled her stuff in the trunk before hopping into the back seat.

They meandered up the coast over the next few days, touring multiple schools. They hit campuses in a whirlwind of brochures, historical monuments, and student unions. Thursday, they reached their destination for the California State Conference, UC Berkeley.

The model UN students rented a house for the week

for both the conference and their school tours in the area. The three of them were offered floor and couch space to stay. Grateful for a few free nights, they camped in the living room in a nest of sleeping bags and earplugs.

CHAPTER 21

While Ganesha and Josie participated in their conference the next day, Carmen took the rail line into San Francisco to meet up with Logan. He had vague ideas about visiting Golden Gate Park, so they met at the nearest rail line stop and meandered toward the park. That was until Carmen realized they were going nowhere near his intended destination and saw him reading the tourist map upside down. She took over navigation after that.

They took a bus to Haight-Ashbury District first. The street teemed with tourists and brightly colored teenage potheads with locks and flowy patchwork clothing. They looked like they came straight out of a deadhead concert.

Inside a boutique secondhand shop full of musty fashionable clothing, Logan lost it over a Members Only bomber jacket with a silky floral-patterned lining. He waxed poetic about it, putting it on immediately and glancing at himself on every reflective surface he passed. With it on, he looked so much like her Logan, the adult

Logan she'd left in 2009, and she longed to reach out and hold his hand.

Instead, she stuffed her hands into her pockets and led them into the park. They rented a couple of bikes and rode them along paths that first cut through open green fields, then up into rolling hills. When they reached the Japanese Gardens nestled within a forest of eucalyptus, they parked their bikes and strolled along verdant path, mesmerized by the miniature bonsai trees, carefully groomed ponds of floating lilies, and swooping architecture. Carmen eventually led them to a coffee shop just past the Japanese Gardens by one of the lakes. They sat with tea and pastries, chatting by the water.

Looking across the lake at boaters, Logan said, "I wish I'd decided to take this trip with friends instead. My dad is driving me crazy. He has nothing good to say about coming here."

"I'm sorry. I wish you could join us for the rest of our road trip, but we're basically done visiting schools now."

"Where have you visited?" he asked.

She ticked them off, then told him about her acceptance letter to San Jose.

"Congratulations! That is so awesome! I'm surprised your mom and dad didn't come to see the school you're going to. Then we could both sit here and complain about our parents."

"I haven't told them yet." Embarrassed for some reason she couldn't name, she avoided eye contact, shredding bread for the birds instead.

"Why not?"

"We're just…" Carmen didn't know how to say that they didn't talk so much as argue. "I'm pretty independent. I just haven't gotten a chance to tell them yet. It's like…

it's like we're roommates instead. It works out pretty well for me most of the time. I don't have a whole lot of rules imposed on me."

"I feel like all I have are rules," he said with a sigh. "My dad has a lot of ideas about what he thinks I should do with my life, and they're exactly what he did. Honestly, the only reason I'm allowed to even consider UCSF is that I got a music scholarship, so he won't have to pay for a lot of it. But it has a bunch of requirements. I'll have to take an intense work-study assignment and get a certain GPA."

"What do you play?" She knew, but it was twenty-seven-year-old Carmen that knew, not seventeen-year-old Carmen.

"I play the piano, the guitar, and the banjo."

"The banjo? Sexy."

"Yeah yeah, I know it's a dorky instrument." He shrugged.

"No, really, I love bluegrass! I was once in Alaska for—" Twenty-four-year-old Carmen had been in Alaska for a travel-nursing assignment. "—to visit family," she amended hastily, waving her hand about vaguely. "And the summers there are so much fun. I think everyone is just so excited because it's sunny outside. All they want to do is play music and drink and have a good time. I went to this bluegrass music festival I stumbled upon along the river in Anchorage. The banjo *is* a sexy instrument. Please tell me you also play the mouth harp."

Logan's expression was that of warm amusement. "God, do I even want to know what that is? You really are full of trivia, Trivia." His gaze lingered, his eye contact making her shy.

"Enough about me," she said, changing the subject,

"tell me about your band. What are you guys called?"

"Don't ask." Logan rolled his eyes heavenward. "We keep changing it. I wanted us to be The Stone Age, but it turns out there's a famous band with nearly the same name. Paul wants the band to be called The Pterodactyls, so we went with that until we realized no one could spell it. Now we're thinking, Rex and Roll."

"What's with the dinosaur obsession?"

Laughing, he looked away from her and across the lake again. "Dinosaurs are cool, okay? Who isn't a little obsessed with dinosaurs?" He took a sip of tea. "Anyway, it's just to get to play more this year. I've played the piano and the banjo since I was a kid. I promised my dad I would cut all extracurriculars to just one subject to concentrate on more academic stuff my senior year. I chose theater, and we're not using music in any of our plays, so I needed to keep playing music somehow. Our band isn't bad, but the other guys aren't serious about music. I think they only agreed 'cause getting to say 'I'm in a band' to girls is a great pickup line. But I want to have a future in music."

"It's great that you know what you want to do with your life."

"Dude, I hope so." He sighed. "My dad always tells me it's a pipe dream, that I'll never make it as a musician. He doesn't want to see me be a starving artist."

Carmen, knowing his future, wanted to tell him it did all work out. She tried to say it as best she could.

"You know," she said, choosing her words carefully. "I've got this idea about success. It's not about how someone else defines it. I think success is being happy and comfortable. If you want to be a musician, be a musician! But that looks different for everyone. You could teach music, write music, play in a band on the weekends and find a day job that pays the bills but doesn't make you miserable."

Carmen, warming to her subject, leaned forward. "I mean, yeah, I could go to school and become a doctor and make a lot more money, but I'd be miserable. I don't want to work crazy long hours, be on-call, and go to school for ten more years. I know I'll be much happier as a nurse. I'll do my job, get to travel, and be in medicine without it being my whole life. Success isn't someone else's definition. It's yours."

She could think of a dozen more examples. She thought of twenty-seven-year-old Ganesha who would find fulfillment by volunteering in political organizations. Josie would find success as a lawyer and a soon-to-be mom. And Logan would find a career in teaching music. She could tell by Logan's pleased smile that she'd made her point.

"Thank you, Trivia. I think I needed to hear that."

That evening, Carmen and Logan met up with Josie and Ganesha at the BART station within walking distance of the theater for *Mamma Mia.* Ganesha positively glowed with smug pride, having taken the club president Craig down a few pegs during their simulated Model UN conference.

"I'm sorry, but Craig was wrong on several points, and if he took offense to me correcting him publicly, that's on him. Plus, he's just a know-it-all, and it felt good to show him that he *doesn't* know it all."

"We're way smarter than him anyway. He's just a rich suck-up." Josie patted Ganesha's back consolingly.

"Yeah." Ganesha sighed. "I'd still take being rich over smart."

"You don't mean that," Carmen said.

"You're right," Ganesha said. "I don't."

With subtle ques, Carmen led them to the theater, Logan still trying and failing to navigate with his tourist map. "Anyway, no one likes Craig. They just hang out with him because of his money. We hang out with each other despite having no money."

"I mean, technically, you guys are hanging out with me because of my dad's money right now," Logan said in a self-deprecating tone.

"Yeah! Thanks for these tickets, by the way!" Ganesha said, faining a bright attatude.

"If it makes you feel any better," Josie said, chiming in, "we wouldn't have come if Craig had invited us to this play."

"That does make me feel better. Thanks for coming, actually. Otherwise, I'd be coming alone. My dad isn't the theater type."

An understatement that Carmen knew all too well.

They enjoyed the play and split up after, with Carmen, Josie, and Ganesha heading back late to the rental house in Berkeley. They were exhausted when they walked up to the house at nearly 1 a.m.

As soon as they walked in, Ganesha groaned. A house party raged at full volume with groups of students scattered about the common areas.

Josie just shrugged and grabbed a beer from the kitchen counter. "When in Rome," she said, then took a swig.

Settling in the loft, they eventually joined in on a game of UNO with students from various high schools. The party attendees were an eclectic mix, with high academic achievement being the major denominator. *Nerds party hard*, Carmen thought with amusement, as the party became progressively louder around them. It didn't look like there would be a free couch to sleep on anytime soon.

Craig came into the room acting drunk. He spotted Ganesha, and though she was across the room, Carmen heard him over the din of the party. "She's not even a very cute lesbian."

Flushed in anger, Carmen looked at Ganesha. Her face was crumpled in horrified recognition.

Her frazzled friend mumbled her subsequent request. "Can we just get out of here? Or go find a room and just hang out?"

Craig must have heard because he leaned over to his friend and laughed. "They're going to go get a room. I wouldn't mind watching that."

Carmen, who was having none of it, said, "What are you talking about, Craig?"

"Oh, are you her girlfriend? Come on, make out, make out!" He cheered and a few people joined in.

"Come on, let's get out of here." Josie stood. "He just wishes someone wanted any action with him, but no one does."

A few people "ooohed" at that.

"No one asked you." He spit the last word in her face.

Josie looked ready to punch him. "You think you're hot, telling girls to make out. Do you think girls kiss girls for guys? That's a joke. If I want to kiss Ganesha, I'll do it because I want to kiss her." And the blonde turned around and did just that. She took Ganesha's face and crushed their lips together.

Several people hollered. One told them to keep going.

For a minute, Ganesha stood immobile, then leaned back, slapped Josie, and stormed out. Josie chased after her and out the door.

Carmen was at a loss. She stood in the room of staring high schoolers for a minute before gathering their bags from the hall closet to follow them out.

Her friends were nowhere in sight by the time she made it through the crowded revelers and out the front door. The minivan was parked down the block where they left it. Glad she had Ganesha's bag, Carmen fished out the keys, got in, and fell asleep in the passenger seat waiting for them.

A knock on the window startled Carmen awake. Wiping a trail of drool from her face, she craned her neck and spotted Josie and Ganesha outside. They weren't yelling at each other, but they were...awkward. She unlocked the doors and rubbed at a crick in her neck. Ganesha wearily flopped down into the driver's seat. "I don't know how you're feeling about it, Carmen, but I want to go home."

Drained from all the drama, Carmen nodded and yawned. "Let's do it. We can be home in seven hours."

"But first, coffee," Josie said.

It was a quiet ride home. Ganesha finally let Carmen drive the car out of exhaustion, and Carmen finished the last leg while the other two slept, listening to the Top 40 on the radio and rocking out on her fourth cup of coffee.

Once she got home, she lugged her stuff down the pathway from the parking lot to her front door, happy to be home. But when she opened the door, she found her dad slumped on the couch with his face in his hands.

"Dad, what's wrong?"

His eyebrows were bunched and the tilt of his mouth downcast. "Anak, I'm sorry, but your mother left. She wants a divorce."

Carmen had not seen it coming this soon. She knew her parents would be better off apart. But knowing it was coming didn't make it any less shocking. And it had come several months earlier than the first time Carmen was seventeen. The last time, her mom had at least given her the option of moving in with her. But her mom hadn't just left her dad or the condo. She'd left the *country.* Her mom just...disappeared while Carmen was out of town.

A deep ache throbbed in her chest, and she felt hollowed out. Her mom hadn't even left a note.

When Carmen retreated to her room, she found an email from her grandmother.

> "Apo, I am so sorry. Your mother has been unhappy for a long time, and she told me she needed to get out of town. She said she needed a ticket to the Philippines, so I bought her one. She's

here with me. If there is anything you
need me to say to her, I will let her
know. I love you, Apo. I'm so sorry."

Her mind a buzz of confusion, Carmen unpacked her
belongings with her limbs on autopilot. She sat at the
dinner table, not sure what to do with herself.

Her dad ordered pizza then laboriously made his way
from the phone to the table. Neither of them was in the
right mindset to make dinner. He sat and stared at her
face, as if searching for something. She stared back. Was
she supposed to cry? Yell? Laugh? She felt...nothing.
Maybe she was in shock. He must not have found what
he was looking for, because he grimaced before looking
away.

"I have a problem, Anak." His voice was hoarse. "I
haven't wanted to admit it for a long time. But your
mother left me because I'm useless and an addict. She
deserved better, and so do you."

"Dad, you were injured at work. It isn't your fault."
Carmen reached over the table and gripped his hand, now
trying to meet his eye. "You've had several surgeries. You
need pain medication. And she left both of us, not just
you." Was she finally angry? Her voice sounded sharp.

"Anak, she loves you. She just couldn't deal with me
anymore."

"She's the one who left. At least you're still *here!*"
Carmen's voice went up an octave, her voice cracking on
the last word.

"I...I'm sorry." His voice wheezed. "She left you, and
it isn't fair."

Carmen felt like breaking something. She preferred
anger to pity. "Dad, can't you be mad at her too? For me?

She's…she has always been a crappy parent, but now she's not even *here* to *be* crappy."

"Honey…" her dad said weakly. "She just…she got sick of me, not you. I need to do better. I need to *be* better."

Carmen's dad quit taking his pain medication that night. He struggled with withdrawals and was so ill that Carmen called out from school and work for several days to help him manage the shaking, nausea, and vomiting. Finally, fearful for his health, she took him to the hospital. After hydrating him with IV fluids in the ER, the doctor referred him to a clinic to safely wean him from the opiates.

When she went back to school, she drifted through her classes, feeling numb to the day-to-day activities.

Maybe because of their trip, or because Carmen was so obviously troubled with family stuff, Ganesha finally seemed to have forgiven her, which Carmen didn't deserve. She treated her as she used to, full of self-deprecating humor and sarcasm in spades.

Or maybe it was because something was going on between Josie and Ganesha now. Something good and happy. They still acted like themselves for the most part. There was no PDA, no flirty talking, but Carmen had been friends with them forever. She could tell. They sat a little closer than before with knees often bumping. And they gave each other these soft fond looks when they thought Carmen wasn't watching.

Several days later, Carmen finally addressed it during lunch in the school cafeteria. "So, are you guys a couple now or something?"

Her friends looked at each other and laughed.

"Or something," Ganesha said.

"I refuse to be defined." Josie raised her hand as if she

was in class. "I'm...into smart. And sassy."

Ganesha's lip tilted up at the compliment, tracing one of the many carvings in the wooden picnic table with a bitten-down fingernail. "You called it first, Carmen. I mean, I don't know how you were so sure I was—gay," Ganesha whispered the last word, her eyes darting up to look at her. "I'm pretty sure I was hiding it from everyone, including myself."

Carmen's grin turned sly. "Maybe I'm from the future and I came back to tell you to stop living a lie. Come out, be proud, it'll all turn out okay!"

"Oh, shut up." But she laughed, then punched Carmen in the arm in what should have been a playful manner but actually hurt.

"Ow!" Carmen rubbed her arm.

Ganesha's expression lacked all sympathy. "I'm still pissed off that you outed me, even if it was an accident. That wasn't cool."

Carmen's teasing smile turned instantly contrite. "I'm sorry, it was truly a horrible thing to do, and I wish I could take it back, or at least take back that I hurt you."

"Thanks." Ganesha looked somewhat mollified by her earnest apology. "It does help your case that it turned out okay for me." And she gave Josie a shy smile.

On Friday, Carmen drove to Mrs. Malone's sprawling ranch-style home for dinner. After their evening meal, they had a date night planned, leaving her to babysit. In the spacious backyard, a dilapidated treehouse sitting in the three-pronged fork of an enormous oak tree caught Carmen's attention.

Her focus brought Mr. Malone's attention to the treehouse. He gestured to it, then set his fork down to sign as he talked. "I built that almost fifteen years ago when we first moved into this house. You can go check it out if you want, but I wouldn't trust the ladder. It's been years since I did any repairs on it."

Carmen praised the craftsmanship and the conversation eventually turned to Carmen.

"You're a senior, right?" Mr. Malone asked. "What are your plans? You already have quite the resume! CPR certified, fluent in sign language—"

"And she may not be my star actor, but she's come up with some pretty interesting additions to our plays this year," Mrs. Malone inserted. "You have her to thank for changing the Piccaninny tribe to Filipino islanders."

"Your costume was beautiful," Alice said.

"My grandmother sent it to me from the Philippines. It's a replica of traditional Filipino clothing."

"Are you Filipino?" Mr. Malone said.

"Yeah, and I plan on studying nursing after I graduate. I know, it's a cliche, a Filipino becoming a nurse." Carmen shrugged one shoulder, self-conscious.

"If it's what you want to do, it doesn't matter if it's a cliche," Mr. Malone said earnestly.

"We're glad you already know so much about taking care of people," Mrs Malone said. "It means you'll be a good babysitter for our daughter. We appreciate it, by the way. We're looking forward to a night out."

Both Mr. and Mrs. Malone smiled at each other.

"Speaking of which, we should get ready to go." Mr. Malone set his silverware down and stood up. "We wrote down a list of important phone numbers and stuck them to the fridge. We'll be home by 10 pm. Alice, we expect you to be in bed by then."

Alice rolled her eyes but agreed.

Gesturing to his daughter, Mr. Malone signed and then spoke, a teasing grin tilting up the corners of his thin lips. "You'll have your hands full with her. She acts like a teenager already."

Once the door had fully closed behind her parents, Alice turned to Carmen. "Finally! I never thought they would leave. It's exhausting having to pretend to be seven years old."

The comment made Carmen laugh. "From what people have said, you haven't been very good at pretending."

"Yeah…. My teachers are all very impressed with their little prodigy," she signed with an exaggerated eye roll. Jumping to the point, she continued. "So, we both woke up in August ten years younger and in 1999 instead of 2009, right?"

"Yes." It was a relief to talk openly about this with someone.

"How did this happen? I should be a seventeen-year-old, not a child."

They traded stories about what the last seven or so months had been like. From her telling, Alice had a lot more trouble adjusting to being seven than Carmen had adjusting to being seventeen.

Unlike Carmen, Alice tried to tell her parents she was a seventeen-year-old, but it hadn't gone well.

"First, they thought I was making up some fantasy, then became concerned and put me in therapy. They're back to thinking it's a story I made up. I only went along with it to get out of therapy. Plus, the one big event I clearly remember from this year is my mom having a stroke. I just couldn't…I couldn't tell them she's going to die. It wouldn't convince them anyway until it happened, and that's precisely what I want to prevent somehow."

Carmen told Alice the list of time-travel theories her online friends helped her come up with and the associated explanations and examples.

"I've crossed off single continuum, fixed points, and time loop, which just leaves infinite timelines. But none of that really helps us, does it?"

With a pensive expression, Alice began signing. She signed slowly, as if thinking over each word deliberately. "I don't know if we can cross off fixed points. Even though your friends ended up together, your parents still separated despite your efforts. Who's to say your friends won't split up one day and end up with the partners you saw at the reunion?" Alice grabbed a pad of paper from a side table and wrote the list down without fixed points crossed off.

1. ~~Single continuum~~
2. Fixed points? Parents still separated. Prevent other bad things from happening.
3. ~~Time loop?~~ It hasn't looped yet. Maybe it still will?
4. Infinite timelines. Most plausible. How to get back to our own?

"I kind of hate the idea that there's nothing big we can change." Carmen didn't want to say it, but they were both thinking specifically of Mrs. Malone's death. If certain significant events were fixed, did that mean she was destined to die?

Wanting to change the subject, Carmen asked about the shared dream they had before their jump backward in time.

"We both must remember the dream, at least a little because you remembered my name. The details are hazy for me, but I recall you asked me what I wanted. The question gave me a panic attack, and I woke up as a teenager."

"The dream was in my backyard, and I was in that treehouse." Alice pointed to it through the window. They were settled in the living room, which looked out at the backyard. The last bit of yellow and orange light from the setting sun lit the treehouse from behind so it was little more than a silhouette. "It's pretty broken down now. In the dream, it looked like how I imagined it would have looked when it was first built—freshly painted with flowers on the windowsill. In real life, I've never actually been up in that treehouse. My parents built it for a child they didn't have for ten years. They had a lot of trouble getting pregnant. They wanted a child for years, and they finally had me. But my mom had a difficult birth, and it's why I'm in a wheelchair. They love me, but I know it's hard on them."

Acutely aware that she was ill-equipped for this conversation, Carmen tentatively offered her opinion, thinking of her mom and her many miscarriages. "Becoming a parent is hard, I think, no matter what. My mom just left my dad and me, and I think she left because she's always been disappointed in our life. When people have children, they have all these hopes and dreams. Some can cope with them not coming true, and some can't. None of us can be perfect children to our parents. I disappoint my mom, but she should still have stuck around." Alice made a sympathetic face.

They stared out at the treehouse and the dark

gathering outside.

Signing slowly, Carmen thought out how to say what she was thinking. "I think...what matters is that your parents love you. I have never gotten the feeling that they're disappointed with you. I got that feeling from my mom *all the time*."

Alice tapped her fingers on the armrest for a few long seconds before responding. "These last few months have reminded me of how much they care about me. I barely remembered my mom. Not the details anyway. She is honestly more incredible than I remembered. Also, more annoying, but that's mostly because she treats me like I'm seven. I've been agonizing over how to save her somehow. I feel like, why else would I have been sent back in time? But I have no idea how to do that. I bug her about her health, but...she doesn't seem unhealthy. I don't know how to save her." Alice gave a defeated shrug, slumped with the impossibility of the situation.

"Do you think so? Do you think we were sent back for a reason?"

"I have to. Why else?"

Carmen thought the same thing herself when she first woke up in 1999. "I have a pretty good life as a twenty-seven-year-old, and this felt like some sort of punishment, being sent back. Maybe this is to remind me of how good I have it? I hated senior year the first time around. I remember feeling so trapped by my life. Socially awkward at school and living with parents who hate each other. But I didn't even manage to stop their divorce. I don't know if I was supposed to, but I've failed. And my mom left the country this time, instead of just my dad."

"What else is different?"

"Everything at this point! I've been living this year thinking about what you said in the dream—when you asked me what I wanted?" Carmen explained the surprise proposal and how terrified it had made her. She backtracked and explained the confusing dynamics of her boyfriend, whom she'd known since high school, but hadn't known the first time she lived through senior year.

"So I've been trying to get to know him again, this version of him because I have no idea if I should say yes. Life was perfect the way it was. Why ruin it with marriage!"

"Why do you think marriage would ruin what you have with Logan? Are you not in love with him?"

"Well yeah, I think so."

"Okay then…"

"I mean, marriage is a big deal! What if we hate each other after a couple of years."

"You mean, like your parents?"

"No, we're nothing like them!" Her shoulders went up in defense, recoiling at the idea.

"I mean, not to get all Freudian, but it's always about your childhood, right?"

"Yeah, but…how do you know this stuff?"

"Since I'm actually a seventeen-year-old applying to college soon, I've watched enough television to get the gist. So, your parents have a rough marriage, which means you're afraid of commitment. Right? Doesn't seem like a crazy leap to make."

It brought a shift in Carmen's head, like a question she hadn't realized she'd asked was being answered. She felt especially stupid for only now making this connection. Having a seven-year-old point it out, even if her mind

208

wasn't seven, was a blow to Carmen's self-esteem. Was she so lacking in self-awareness that she hadn't seen it until now?

"It's hard to see the forest for the trees." Alice gave her a pat on the shoulder.

Carmen had never seen the idiom signed before, but it was a visual amalgam of confusion, tree, and forest, which were similar signs, except the trees multiplied. It had the same general meaning though. It was difficult to see the whole of a situation when you were enmeshed in the details.

They went out to the dark treehouse to investigate. Both suspected nothing strange or magical would happen, but it couldn't hurt to return to the site of their shared dream. Carmen climbed the rickety ladder until one rung snapped under her weight. She barely caught herself from tumbling to the ground below. It took a moment to calm her racing heart before she pushed up the trick floor. Sadly, she found only spiders and dust.

Back inside, they dug around the bathroom cabinets to see if Alice's mom was on any mysterious medications. They found nothing but vitamins. They traded screen names on AOL so they could chat unobserved, and Carmen quickly helped Alice to bed when they heard the Malones' car pulling into the driveway.

Thanking her, they gave her more money than she expected and sent on her way.

When Carmen arrived at home, her dad slept in his recliner. He and Carmen had been slowly packing the condo up to put it on the market. Without her mom's income, they wouldn't be able to afford the mortgage. They planned on getting a small apartment until Carmen went to college, then her dad would decide what to do.

Carmen's bitterness still simmered below the surface. This wasn't a new feeling, just amplified. They had never seen eye to eye. But she also felt more sympathy than she ever had before. Her grandmother had shown her that. She now understood her mom's motivations, although it did nothing to assuage her anger.

Carmen didn't *want* to sympathize with her mom right now. She needed to stay angry. It was easier than the hollow pit that threatened to override it.

CHAPTER

23

Weeks passed. Carmen soldiered on. They sold the condo. She and her dad moved into a tiny apartment he could afford on his disability. He slept on his recliner in the living room, giving her the privacy of the one bedroom.

Her dad's physical therapy was slow but showing steady progress. He joined an anonymous sobriety group for prescription drug abuse. The doctor prescribed him non-opioid pain relief medication instead. He started swimming at the Y. When he got clearance from his surgeon, he got a part-time job working as a taxi driver. It was the first job he'd felt well enough to work in years.

Logan invited her to one of his band's concerts. He was dressed in the silk-gray Member's Only jacket on stage, and while he wouldn't be combing his hair back into a bun anytime soon, he started growing it out enough that he no longer had straight-from-boot-camp hair. He looked so much like her quirky self-assured adult Logan that she wanted to reach out and touch him..

She was pretty sure she swooned through the entire set. She loved watching him on stage, he had such frenetic energy. After they finished and packed up their gear, Logan joined her, Josie, and Ganesha in the audience for the next set.

"They're our main competition," Logan said, gesturing to the band on stage, "and they've got *years* on us." His warm breath ghosted across her ear as he spoke. She shivered.

"You shouldn't sell yourself short." She glanced over her shoulder at him. "You can really rock out on that hillbilly guitar."

Logan's eyes widened in mock hurt. "Hillbilly guitar? I've never heard it called that before."

"Come on, no one plays the banjo to pick up ladies." She smirked at him. "You're lucky I like the hillbilly guitar."

"Oh, so if I tried to pick you up, you'd be into it?"

"Only if you're playing the hillbilly guitar," she said with a teasing lilt, though he stood awfully close.

"I'll remember that." A smile curled at the edge of his mouth, showing a hint of teeth with his canines.

It was crowded toward the front, so he stood closer through the next song. She swore she could feel the warmth of him through her thin shirt, very aware of the little space between her back and him. If she leaned back just a little, she felt she might break the tension between them. She was just working up the courage to turn to look up at him again when she saw a familiar face in the crowd to her left. Just as Carmen spotted her, so did Josie, who called to her.

"Kelly!" Josie waved her arm dramatically over

people's heads, causing several people to turn and look.

Kelly spotted them and looked for a moment as if she would rather pretend she hadn't seen them.

Way to go, making this super awkward, Josie!

"Hey, guys! What a coincidence seeing you here! I, um, really like the music."

Nodding along, Carmen felt that Logan had pulled away, the heat of his chest disappearing.

"Hey, Kelly."

She gave him a cool hello, before turning back to Josie.

"Anyway, I should really get going. Just coming back from the bathroom to find my friends—see you later, guys." She disappeared into the crowd with another wave.

"Well, that was awkward," Logan said.

"Yup," Ganesha said.

"Oh, I'm sorry!" Josie said, likely only then realizing how uncomfortable she'd made everyone by dragging Kelly over to say hi.

The band on stage wound down for their last song, and the crowd thinned, which meant Logan no longer stood as close as he had been. Carmen couldn't find the courage to close the distance, Kelly having broken the moment. Carmen silently cursed Josie in her head when they split from Logan at the end of the show, only a platonic wave as her parting gift.

When Carmen got home that night, she was greeted with an email from @BearyFunny.

> "My story is being published! The agency is in Los Angeles, and I'm flying in next weekend to complete some paperwork. Please come meet me?"

Carmen was overjoyed for her. This wouldn't happen for years yet in Carmen's original timeline. The next day at school, Carmen asked Josie and Ganesha if they wanted to join her, but they had a big exam Monday and weren't free. She was glad anyway. She never actually explained her blog or her online community of friends to them and didn't want to explain it now. This was still the year 2000, and "online friends" usually equated to pervy catfishers.

Carmen planned on going alone until Logan mentioned that his band was playing at an all-ages club in the greater L.A. area.

"I'd love it if you came," he said during the break between classes. "Can we drive up together?" His eyes lingered on hers.

Lately, everything between them felt laden with something more, making her suddenly shy. She tucked her hair behind an ear and broke eye contact to look down. "Yeah...actually, I've got plans myself in L.A. if you don't mind dinner with a friend from out of town beforehand?"

CHAPTER
24

Carmen had Logan all to herself during the drive to L.A. Since the backseat was full to the brim with music equipment, Logan's bandmates drove in a second vehicle following them. They drove the first half with the windows thrown wide open. The wind mussed her hair into a whirlwind of curls that she spent the second half of the drive detangling with her fingers. She wasn't sure if the sunset was playing tricks on her, but the sky's pinks and yellows and purples were bright electric, with L.A.'s dark skyline soft and shadowy. It had a surreal feel and looked more like pop art than real life. She regretted not bringing her sketchbook and committed the sight to memory for later.

Despite her initial reluctance, Carmen told Logan all about her blog and online community of friends. She couldn't figure out another way to explain why she was meeting with a mid-thirties' woman from across the country.

"Trivia, you just got cooler in my book. I'm not much of a reader, but I'll read your fanfiction! Is it sexy fanfiction?"

"Stop! This is so embarrassing!" She hid in the neck of her pullover.

Laughing, he pulled the neck down, only glancing over briefly as he drove. She felt his hand brush her neck, and it made her flush. Was it just her, or did his hand linger for a moment longer?

"Come on, I mean it!" he said, more earnest now. "I'll read it if you write it, I promise."

"I don't write fanfiction. I edit and draw for my friends mostly. They'll write a story, and I'll draw a scene or the cover for them, or I'll take a scene from canon and draw it."

"I had no idea you were an artist!"

"I'm not an artist," she said, abashed. "I just like drawing."

"I'm not a musician then. I just like music." His voice was heavy with sarcasm.

"Okay fine, I like to draw."

"Have you taken art classes?"

"I used to, but I don't really like drawing what other people tell me to draw. It's just a hobby. Not like music is for you."

He gave a non-committal hmmm.

They arrived in L.A. as the sun set, the sky turning dark and purple as they unloaded the equipment from the car into the back of the grimy club. Once they were done, they drove over to the Dim-Sum restaurant she and @BearyFunny, AKA Francis, had picked for their dinner meeting.

Francis was just as Carmen remembered her, tall

and willowy at nearly six feet with dark skin and a shaved head. She wore colorful dangling earrings that brushed her shoulders. They hugged, and Carmen made introductions as they seated themselves.

"So, Carmen tells me that she edited your story?" Logan fumbled with his chopsticks, trying, and failing to scoop a dumpling he accidentally dropped into his sauce. His lips twisted into a moue of concentration so familiar to her from their many half-remembered moments together. It made Carmen heartsick. A lock of his hair fell over his eyes, and she wanted to reach forward and smooth it back. She tucked her hands under her thighs instead.

"Yeah, she's been editing for me for the last year or two." Francis's warm and honeyed Southern drawl made her instantly likable. "And she draws the cover art for my stories. I've got some printed here if you want to see them?" Carmen groaned as Francis pulled a folder out of her messenger bag.

"Carmen." Francis tsked. "You really should be proud of your work. I wanted to talk to you about it." She passed the folder to Logan to look through but addressed Carmen. "The publishing agency saw your work and may want to use it for the actual cover art."

Logan held up one printout, a comic book style cover she'd done, heavily influenced by mid-century pop art, all stippled dots and bold line-work, with bright splashes of color.

"I can see why. This is very cool, Trivia. Don't sell yourself short." He looked at her with a lift to his eyebrow, impressed.

"If you're willing, Carmen," Francis said, and Carmen's attention shifted to her. "They'll want a contract signed, and you'll get paid for the work."

She was very interested. Carmen flushed with both embarrassment and pride.

At the end of their meal, her soon-to-be-published friend promised to pass her email along to the right people and insisted on paying for dinner. Then after parting hugs, they left for Logan's show.

On the drive over, Logan looked to be mulling his words over carefully. "Remember that pep talk you gave me about success and how it looks different for people? Maybe you should take your own advice."

Carmen pondered this as they drove.

"You know, I just… Art is something I do when I have free time." She'd always loved art and being creative when she was younger, but she gave it up like so many other hobbies she felt had no place in her adult life.

"I don't…" Carmen tried to think of how to say this without insulting Logan, who planned on pursuing a career in the arts. "I don't have a high threshold for uncertainty. I like to be sure of where my next paycheck is coming from." Carmen tried to think of how else to explain herself. "My…my family is… We struggle a lot, financially. And I guess I feel like unless it's going to make me money, I don't want to trust that it will earn me a living. I could never be self-employed."

She was content to be a nurse and felt fulfilled by it. But…she could do art too. She didn't have to be paid to do something she liked. However, Francis's unexpected offer had given her a confidence boost. Her art could be something that other people liked too.

"A wise woman told me to do what makes me happy," Logan said. "Art makes you happy. And it's good enough that people may want to give you money for it. Just saying."

Carmen laughed, rolling her eyes as he paraphrased what she said to him in San Francisco. "Fine, yes, I should listen to my own advice."

When they arrived at the all-ages club, Carmen got herself a soda while Logan and his band prepared their equipment. They were opening for another band that must have been a lot more "punk" and a lot less "emo" than Logan's band, the Rexinators—another iteration of their dinosaur-themed naming scheme.

Maybe punk was the wrong word. Metal? There was certainly a lot of metal in the faces of the gathering crowd, and lots of black and leather too.

When Logan and his band started, Carmen could tell they had picked tonight's set for this crowd. The music they played was full of feverish energy she hadn't heard from them before. A mosh pit of people formed around her, bumping into each other with increasing vigor. She attempted to escape the circle of people, trying to find a part of the crowd less enthusiastic about violence. An exceptionally energizing chorus started, and the group went nuts. An elbow caught her under her left eye, and she went down, slipping in someone's soda. She had the presence of mind to cover her head as she hit the ground, feet stomping all around her.

The music abruptly went out, and Logan jumped into the audience, yelling for people to get out of the way. Someone helped her up just as Logan made it to her side, his face full of concern. He reached forward and tilted her chin up, inspecting the damage.

"Trivia! Are you okay?"

Her injured eye watered, but despite the pain, Carmen laughed, with Logan still holding her face.

"Just my pride is hurt."

His finger brushed across the bruise forming on her cheek, and she winced.

"Ouch, okay, my pride and my face."

His eyes flickered down to her lips, and Carmen wasn't sure if he leaned forward, or she did, or they both gravitated toward each other. But it was undeniable and inevitable. She felt a warm puff of air on her face before their lips met, insistent and without hesitation. His mouth was hot and warm and electric. He threaded his fingers into her hair and tilted her head up and to the side to deepen the kiss, and she gasped. As if some dam had broken, some unseen barrier had collapsed, they pulled into each other. However, the banjo strapped to his front stopped them, and she pulled away, breathless.

"I've wanted to do that for a while," he said, looking down at her wet mouth with a smile on his.

"Yeah?" she said with a sigh.

Pulled in for another kiss, she let him take control, melting into his embrace. Logan pulled away as one of his bandmates hollered. "Oi! Loverboy — there is a time and a *place*, and mid-show is not it! Get back up here!"

The surroundings snapped back into focus, and she realized the audience around them was cheering them on. The music had stopped as their lead singer made out with her.

He laughed, a joyful bark of noise. He kissed her quickly before bounding back onstage. She relocated to the back of the audience with an ice pack pressed to her face. For the following few songs, she listened in a haze of warm feelings.

He sang with exuberance she hadn't seen yet and looked at her with stars in his eyes.

After their set, Logan found her in the crowd. He picked her up and spun her around, her squealing. He kissed her again, and he tasted like soda, and home.

"I've wanted to do that for a while," he said into her lips.

Laughing, she pulled away. "So you said."

"You're pretty cool, Trivia."

"I've always thought so, but few agree."

"I find that hard to believe. I also find it hard to believe we just met this year. I feel like we've always known each other."

His comment and the fact that this was true, made her laugh. They had known each other longer, but it had always felt that way. They just clicked. Carmen hadn't been sure that would be true of this younger version of Logan, whom she had only known as popular and unapproachable at seventeen. But that wasn't true of most people—the idea that people were "popular" or "unapproachable" or whatever. People were not just the labels they were given, and no one was genuinely so strange that they couldn't be understood.

Her mom briefly entered her thoughts. She had always painted her as the bad guy in her life. However, after learning more about her mom's history, she understood her more. But thoughts of her mom quickly left her as Logan leaned forward and kissed her again.

He gazed into her eyes. "I just didn't... I wanted to make sure you knew this wasn't some rebound. I like you a lot. Seeing your art today, and the work you put into the plays, and your random knowledge, and your crazy ideas. I think you're one of the weirdest girls I've ever met."

"What?" she said, offended.

"I'm into it, Trivia. I'm really, really into it." Laughing, he buried his fingers in her hair and kissed her again.

"I just feel lucky to know you."

His smile widened, his dimple making its presence known. "Reminds me of that song."

"Song?" She felt a pulse of déjà vu.

"You know, that song every band likes to cover." He started humming, his voice quiet but rich and warm.

> *"Lucky to have her,*
> *Lucky, she has you.*
> *With a winning hand at poker,*
> *I'd still bet on you.*
> *If I walked by a four-leaf clover,*
> *I'd always pick you.*
> *I'd choose a life sober,*
> *than a day without you..."*

Their song. He was quoting their song to her. Her mind was buzzing and warm with memory.

She was on cloud nine when she got home late that night. Then the feeling came crashing down at the sight of her dad asleep on the couch. Not everything was aligning for her, as her home situation attested to. She thought about emailing her lola to send a message to her mom, but Carmen was still so *angry*. She wrote on her blog instead.

> "Things have been so busy and tumultuous, and I just haven't had much spare time to reflect. My friendships are finally on the mend.

I got into the school I wanted on a full ride. The guy I like, likes me back! And @BearyFunny is getting her story published! The agency may even use my cover art!

"But my mom left. As in, she fled the country altogether while I was visiting schools. She didn't leave a note. She just disappeared. And I'm just so angry. But the part that makes me angriest is that I knew this was coming. I knew she was unhappy. My parent's marriage… it hasn't been good…ever. She was right to leave him, as much as I hate to admit that because he's always been a great father to me. But she was miserable with him, and I knew it. She had an addict for a husband and had to work twice as hard to pay the bills. So I get why she would leave him.

"But she left me too. And I've always acted like I didn't need her, but I guess I do. Because it feels like a part of me is missing. I thought catching the interest of the guy I liked was what I needed, and tonight he kissed me. And guys, IT WAS MAGICAL. But it still doesn't fill that hollowed-out part that she left. So I don't know why I'm pouring my heart out to the internet, but I got the message clear as day from her. No letter, no phone number, no email since she left. She wants nothing to do with me."

CHAPTER 25

As Carmen exchanged books at her locker, someone came up from behind and tapped her shoulder. When she looked, no one was there, so she turned the other way to find Logan with a big toothy grin on his face.

"Got ya."

"I take it back." Carmen rolled her eyes. "You aren't funny."

"You thought I was funny? Thanks!" He was like a puppy, excitable and happy to be with her.

"Not anymore," she said mock-seriously.

"Knock knock," he said in a singsong voice.

"A knock-knock joke isn't going to convince me either," she said. "That's on par with the old tap on the other shoulder trick. Are you five?"

"Knock knock." He insisted.

She lifted an eyebrow at him. "Fine. Who's there?"

"Cows go."

"Cows go, who?" she said as she pulled books from

her locker.

"No, Trivia, they go MOO."

A laugh burst out of her, despite her best efforts. "That is *such* a bad joke. I didn't know I was signing up for this kind of torture." He pulled her books away to carry them for her as she continued speaking. "Have your jokes always been this bad?"

They were always that bad. Seventeen-year-old and twenty-seven-year-old Logan both had a fondness for '50s sitcom dad jokes. But she liked this game of him being silly and her acting long-suffering. They walked down the hallway toward the theater classroom.

"You wound me! Okay, Trivia, you want to be all intellectual? I was doing the crossword this morning — What's a six-letter word for perfect?"

She thought for a minute, then said, "Intact?"

"Carmen." He gave her his wolfish grin.

She loved his stupid handsome face. She kissed him just before entering the theater classroom.

Self-conscious, Carmen walked into the class they shared with Kelly, hand in hand. She was sure they had dopey grins on both their faces. Kelly only gave them a brief look before turning back to the conversation she had been involved in with Jessie, the fellow cheerleader who'd given Logan grief after Kelly and Logan's breakup. Kelly seemed to take it in stride, no surprise or jealousy on her face, just casual interest. In high school, weeks were like years, and Kelly didn't seem phased by the apparent new development between Carmen and Logan.

Carmen watched Mrs. Malone closely in theater class, in Society, and cross-country. No signs of illness. Carmen even weirded out Mrs. Malone during a meet that week when she encouraged her to cut back on the caffeine and energy drinks again and asked her if she had a history of smoking.

"Between you and my daughter, I'll never have any peace. Just as a reminder, Ms. Santos, *I* am the adult." Mrs. Malone's rebuke had a joking edge, but Carmen took the hint.

She and Alice kept in touch online, but neither of them had a hint as to what to do as the end of the year drew ever closer.

Senioritis set in fast for everyone as they prepared for end of year exams. During one of the last Society rehearsals, dressed up as the Scarecrow for dress rehearsal, Logan jumped up on stage as she and much of the club were working on various props or rehearsing. He held his banjo and started strumming and humming. He played this disgustingly sappy song that had been playing on all the radio stations, a twangy country song about high school sweethearts. A banner dropped down behind him that said, "Prom?"

It was so cheesy and so perfectly Logan. Here he was, with a prom-posal. It wasn't in the gym, he wasn't holding a ring, and their song wasn't playing. Instead, the song he sang was so terrible she couldn't help but cringe and laugh — likely his goal. But it certainly called to mind another kind of proposal that would happen on these school grounds. If only he knew.

"You said you liked the hillbilly guitar," he said once he finished the song and jumped down from the stage to cheers. "So, I figured you couldn't say no to this." And he plucked the banjo as one would dramatically play the air guitar.

"You are simply irresistible in those silly overalls." She pulled him forward by those said overalls to kiss him.

Before they made more of a scene, Mrs. Malone called attention. "Okay, great performance. Thank you, Logan. No kissing during school-related activities. Back to work, everyone."

They pulled away from each other with warm cheeks. Carmen realized she'd never not been sure of Logan.

"Yes," she said simply to Logan and smiled at him before returning to painting the backdrop she'd been working on. Her *yes* had weight to it, and she realized she was saying it to this Logan and her future Logan.

She had been filled with so much...fear for the future. Fear of his proposal and marriage and the idea of being tied down by another person. But she realized gradually over the past year that marriage was just a document to prove you would continue to choose the other person you were with. It wasn't a prison sentence to marry someone. Love had always frightened her. Being in love felt like an exposed wire, letting someone have the ability to hurt you at any time, abandon or judge or even disappoint you. And love could lead to all those things.

But it didn't have to be something to fear. Logan had never given her any indication that he was anything less than fascinated with her in the future or now.

Relationships weren't about...leashes and losing a part of yourself as she had sometimes unconsciously feared. It was about...choosing to be with the person you were with, over and over and over again.

That night when she got home, she wrote another journal entry.

> "I got asked to prom tonight, and
> I said yes. Logan is...he's good and
> kind, and he makes me happy. But for

so long, I've felt like I've been holding him at arm's length, scared to get closer. Commitment has always frightened me. But Logan is worth saying yes to. He's worthy of trust, I think.

"I've always been afraid of commitment because I had only bad examples of relationships around me. I knew from a young age that my parents were not happy with each other. My mom has been a constant nag to my dad and me — always wanting perfection, wanting us to be different than we are. But my dad and I haven't made it easy on her either. I've always thought the worst of her, so she gave me the worst. I wish I'd been kinder to my mom. Even if she was sometimes difficult to get along with, she deserved kindness. But talking to my lola this Christmas made me realize how much she's suffered. And yes, she could have been a better mom, but I could have done better too at being her daughter. I resolve to be better to all the people I care about. To my parents, to Logan, to my friends."

That evening, after closing her computer, she checked the time and rushed to get ready. They were going to a football game that night. Very little of her future knowledge had been helpful or panned out, but she remembered a specific prank and wanted to see it herself. Carmen made sure to drag Logan, Ganesha, and Josie to the game.

"I had no idea you were a fan of football, Trivia," Logan said, juggling their drinks as they sat down.

"Oh yeah, I mean, I don't really understand sports, but live sports are fun. Sorry I never watched any of your matches, Logan." The water polo season had been over since March, which gave Logan more free time. Carmen was not a football fan, but she wanted to see the drama unfold.

They cheered for their school, her friends making running commentary of how terrible both teams were and gorged on snacks and soda. On cue, a silver SUV drove through the field at halftime and ran into a ditch on the other side of the arena. The game ended early, and the police were called. But the crowd went wild, cheering and doing the wave for the driver, who ran across the field, dodging campus security and the referee. Naked.

It was the best football game she'd ever been to.

CHAPTER
26

The end of Carmen's senior year drew ever closer. The
last play came for her with much less fanfare than the
previous two. Carmen had tried out for the Wicked
Witch, but the part went to a more experienced senior.
Instead, she got the bitty role of the Wicked Witch's
sister, who gets crushed by Dorothy's house in one of the
first scenes. Carmen's only line was one long scream at
the beginning. Still, Carmen played her role each night
with gusto. Logan said her blood-curdling screech gave
him the heebie-jeebies, which was her intention. So, all
in all, Carmen was happy to do it. After they took their
bows, Carmen met with Mr. Malone and Alice at their
seats. She was chatting and signing with them when Mrs.
Malone came up.

"Wonderful job, Carmen. I think this was your
loudest, shrillest cry yet. I don't even know if you needed
the mic."

"Thanks, Mrs. Malone," Carmen said, smiling in

satisfaction. "It was a pleasure."

"Are your parents here?" Mrs. Malone asked, looking around. "I'd like to ask them to dinner and thank them for raising such an accomplished daughter."

For no discernable reason Carmen felt embarrassed. "Oh…my dad had to work and uh…my mom is…well, I haven't seen her."

Mrs. Malone lifted an eyebrow in question, but likely sensing Carmen's resistance to discussing the topic, she dropped it. "Listen, would you like to have a celebratory dinner at our house tonight? You can invite Logan too. I'd love to have some of my favorite seniors over before you all leave for the great big outside world."

"Thank you, that would be lovely. I'll ask him." Thinking of the logistics, she said, "He doesn't know sign language, though."

"That's okay," Alice said. "Mom and Dad are used to interpreting for me."

Threading through the crowd to find her people, Carmen first found Josie and Ganesha, who often came to her last showing. They said it was most likely to be the best of the three nights, and they weren't wrong.

"Thanks so much for coming, guys!"

"Of course," Josie said.

"We wouldn't miss it," Ganesha said.

"Hey, listen, I know I said I was free, but Mrs. Malone invited me over for dinner, and I feel like it would be rude to say no."

"That's cool. We can find our own dinner plans," Josie said quickly.

They smiled at each other, and it was a private, just-for-each-other kind of smile that just screamed "couple." Most of the time, Carmen forgot her two best friends were dating each other because they acted much as they always had. But she could see it in the occasionally shared smiles, the sitting slightly closer than they would have previously. Her friends were very private. Or at least, the high school versions of them were. Adult Ganesha, likely compensating for her years of being in the closet, had become very comfortable with public displays of affection. Still, that content smile shared between them gave Carmen a warm, fluttery feeling in her chest to see them happy. She would never have seen it coming, but now she wondered how she could have missed it. They were a cute couple.

Carmen went and asked Logan if he was interested in dinner. He was still in costume and hadn't brought a change of clothes, so he and Carmen dropped by his place so he could get changed. When they went inside, Logan's dad and stepmom sat on the couch watching TV.

"Hello, Mr. and Mrs. Sardino," Carmen greeted as they briefly passed the living room.

Logan's dad didn't even look up from the television. "Hello, Kelly," he said vaguely as he took a sip of his beer.

Ouch.

"Dad, it's Carmen." Logan looked both pained and embarrassed at once.

He had the good grace to look a little embarrassed and finally looked up at her from the couch. "Yeah, sorry, Carmen."

Logan ushered her upstairs and apologized once they were alone in his room. "I'm sorry, he's a jerk."

Carmen, agreeing but not wanting to seem rude, shrugged and smiled reassuringly at him. "It's fine. Let's just get ready and go."

Logan dug through his closet, then, not finding what he was looking for, excused himself to run downstairs to the laundry.

Walking around his room, she looked at what he had on display. The room was clean for a teenage boy, which wasn't surprising to Carmen. She had lived with the adult Logan and knew he was a very tidy person, unlike her. A keyboard stood in the corner with his banjo hung up above it, and neat stacks of sheet music rested on its top. There was a bookcase with swim and water polo trophies. His ROTC uniform, which he wore to school on Fridays, hung on his closet door, pressed and fresh-looking. He also had some signed band posters framed on his walls. His room screamed teenage Logan, a mix of the many after-school activities he was involved in. It made her smile to see it all.

At raised voices, she went toward the door, which was cracked a sliver, to eavesdrop. She couldn't see them but could hear voices coming from the bottom of the staircase.

"Dad, I don't want to talk about this right now. I'm in a hurry."

"The deadline for signing up is in a couple of days, and you can still apply," Logan's dad said, his gruff voice loud and urgent. "The Reserves will still let you go to that school of yours. You just have to commit to one weekend a month and two weeks a year."

Logan's voice was firm and clipped in response. "I am not going to sign up. I'm sorry, but it's not in me."

"I fought for this country, and you won't do the same?" His dad roared, louder still.

"I'm going upstairs, Dad—"

"It's that girl you're dating now," Logan's dad said

234

in a nasty tone. "I don't know why you're not with the other girl. She was a girl you could bring home to the family. She—"

"You just liked Kelly because she agreed with you," Logan said, interrupting him with a quiet but cold tone. "If you liked her so much, why don't you date her."

Logan was in sight suddenly, walking up the stairs and away from his dad, a stack of laundry in his hands and a thunderous expression on his face. Carmen quickly ducked away from the door and busied herself checking out his sheet music. He came into the room and had mostly wiped the angry expression off his face, although he was quieter than he had been.

He went into the bathroom to change, then they left the house. Carmen was glad his parents disappeared from the living room so she wouldn't have to see and talk to them.

They got into Carmen's car as she knew the way. It was a quiet drive out of the neighborhood before Logan spoke up.

"You heard some of that?" He looked over at her, but she kept her eyes on the road.

"Yeah..." Carmen was embarrassed for him and herself.

"I'm sorry, he's really a jerk. I promise, I inherited my personality from my mom. And her good looks."

"It's really okay..." Carmen had made her peace with his dad or at least made peace with the fact that they would never see eye to eye.

"It's not. I'm sorry you heard any of that. But truthfully, I'm glad he disapproves of you."

Carmen gave him a look.

"No." He rushed to explain at her offended expression.

"I mean, he's got questionable taste. I'm not him. We don't like the same things. So, if he doesn't like you, it probably means you're perfect for me." She could see an apologetic look on his face as he looked over at her.

Carmen couldn't hold his family against him without being a hypocrite. Her mom was no treat — she knew that. And while future Logan and Carmen's dad got along well, which was ideal because Carmen's dad was over nearly every other weekend, he was a reformed-drug addict with money issues. He was forever borrowing from adult Carmen.

Things were never simple or easy. It would have been great if Logan's dad wasn't misogynistic and rude, and both their moms hadn't left them behind, but those were the cards they'd been dealt.

"It really is okay, Logan. My mom probably wouldn't approve of you, but she doesn't like me much either, so…" She shrugged.

Logan reached over and held her free hand as she drove.

Maybe because he had been vulnerable, she wanted to confess to her family troubles. They'd only been dating a short while, but she hadn't brought her mom up until now. She hadn't wanted to taint their new relationship's fresh, happy nature. But she knew he would understand because she already knew him, knew his history, and knew he would appreciate her confiding in him and likely feel closer to her for this shared hurt.

"She just up and left while I was out of town on our spring break trip. She booked a flight to the Philippines, and I haven't heard a word from her since."

"Wow, I'm sorry." Logan squeezed her hand. "I know that's a poor response, but that sucks."

"She…" Carmen didn't know how to talk about this — about the tangle of guilt and anger in her. "She has never been happy, married to my dad. But she just…left. Left me, and I know I'm nearly an adult, but I keep wracking my brain over what I did that made her leave me too."

He paused as if debating if he should share too. "It's not comparable, but my mom left the country too. She raised me after my parents divorced when I was a baby, but she remarried, and her new husband got a new job in Indonesia, of all places." He played with her fingers as he said this, staring out the passenger window in thought.

"What was I supposed to do?" he continued. "Start high school in a foreign country? So, my brother and I moved in full-time with our dad a couple of years ago. We always spent summers with him, but…we're very different people. And he wants us to be little carbon copies of him, and we're…not. Still, you should know that their opinions don't determine our worth. I'm sorry she left, but it's not your fault."

When they parked at Mrs. Malone's house, Logan leaned over and gave her a kiss, his hands in her hair.

She was ready to put the whole conversation behind them. "Let's have a nice night, yeah? Forget all about our complicated families?"

A smirk formed on his lips. "I can be distracting." He leaned forward, and she lost herself in the warmth of his mouth and his hands. They walked up to Mrs. Malone's door later than they planned, mussed from kissing and sappy smiles on their faces.

After a late dinner, Carmen joined Mrs. Malone in the kitchen to help wash dishes. Mr. Malone and Alice were trying to teach Logan the sign alphabet with some success in the living room.

"Thanks a lot for dinner," Carmen said. "It was delicious."

"Of course, I'll miss the two of you when you graduate this year. I've had Logan all four years, but I'm glad you decided to join us this year in the theater. And having a babysitter for Alice is such a treat."

"She's a smart girl, and she's pretty independent," Carmen said. "She makes it easy on me."

Mrs. Malone looked into the living room at her daughter, and her face softened. "She is very self-sufficient, as long as things are within reach and wheelchair accessible. But things are never easy for her. I wish she didn't have an uphill battle with *everything*. Just navigating a grocery store can be nearly impossible for her if it's not accessible. If it was just the mobility issue or just being deaf... I just wish the world was more accessible to her. We tried getting her cochlear implants, but her neurologist nixed the idea because of her seizures. And now that she's older, she hates the idea of hearing aids. She says her deafness and her wheelchair are not disabilities, they give her a community and mobility. She's *so* scary smart. Her teachers are encouraging me to move her up a grade, but I just don't know. She has trouble getting along with her classmates, and I worry that moving her up will isolate her even more. I just don't know what to do."

"Being a parent sounds difficult," Carmen said, trying to sympathize.

"Yeah," Mrs. Malone said. "It's funny to hear that from a kid, but you're not wrong."

It probably was a little weird coming from a teenager. Carmen laughed at herself "I just mean, I've been thinking about this a lot lately. I don't have the best relationship with my mom." Carmen's face pulled into a frown. She looked down at the dish she was drying so she wouldn't have to look at Mrs. Malone. "My parents are getting separated, and she just left one day, and I haven't seen her since." It looked like Carmen would be talking about this with everyone today. "But you're still here, and that's what matters."

"I'm sorry about that, Carmen," Mrs. Malone said with a downturned mouth. "No parent should leave their child by choice."

"Yeah...but I haven't been the best daughter either. I know she's got her own stuff she's dealing with, and I haven't been the most understanding or sympathetic."

"Yeah, but she's the adult. Carmen, you're a good kid. I'm sure whatever she's dealing with, she'll reach out to you eventually."

Even though Carmen was twenty-seven on the inside, she still hadn't responded particularly well to her mom this time around either. Had she somehow pushed her away sooner? Carmen's mom went all the way to the Philippines to get away from Carmen and her dad. Mrs. Malone put a comforting hand on her shoulder before crossing the kitchen.

"Come on, let's pull the cookies out of the oven and go save Logan from those two." She stumbled halfway across the kitchen, going down to one knee.

"Mrs. Malone!" Carmen rushed to help her up.

Her husband called out from the living room. "Everything okay?"

The older woman shook her head, holding it with one hand. "I'm sorry, I got a little dizzy. I've been having terrible migraines lately."

Carmen looked over the kitchen island to the living room at Alice, who had a worried look on her face, having witnessed the stumble.

"You should go have yourself checked out," Carmen said, urging her teacher.

"I have an appointment next week," Mrs. Malone said, waving her off. "I'll let them know. But I've had migraines all my life. Sometimes they're just triggered by lack of sleep or certain food."

Carmen looked at the clock. It was nearing 10 p.m. It was past time for them to leave so the Malones could get some rest.

They had cookies, Mrs. Malone wincing at the light from the living room lamps. Feeling they had overstayed their welcome, despite reassurances to the contrary, Carmen and Logan made their goodbyes and headed home. Worry gnawed at Carmen, and she spent too much time tossing and turning that night, fearing history would repeat itself.

CHAPTER 27

The morning of the last meet of the year for cross-country dawned warmer than 5 a.m. should be. Carmen slept terribly the night before, plagued by fears about the day. She and Alice emailed a lot over the last week about Alice's mom. Her doctor's appointment came and went with little fanfare, according to Alice. She nagged at her mom to tell her about it, but Mrs. Malone hadn't said anything concerning, only that imaging was ordered.

In Carmen and Alice's original timeline, today was the day Mrs. Malone would have some sort of stroke while running. Alice and Carmen had no idea how to stop it. Alice said in her last email that she threw an absolute fit the night before, crying and begging her mom not to come, saying she had a bad feeling about today. The elder Malone had been shaken up by Alice's extreme reaction to the race, but insisted she was still coming. She finally promised she wouldn't run in the race with the team as she usually did and would only supervise from the sidelines.

Today's race was against Jenny's school, so Carmen showed up at St. Mary's early to meet Jenny. She picked up her racing bib, then found her in the milling crowd. Her friend wore her school's colors, red and gold, and was fixing her ponytail as Carmen walked up.

"Carm! Glad we finally get to race against each other. We're going to clean the floor with your team."

"That sounds unsanitary," Carmen said, bending down to tighten her shoelaces.

Her words only made Jenny groan. "You won't even do me the favor of some classic race trash-talking?"

"That also sounds unsanitary," Carmen deadpanned.

Laughing, Jenny rolled her eyes. "I guess your version of psyching me out is just to mildly annoy me with bad jokes? It's working."

During their stretch, Jenny kept a running commentary of school gossip while Carmen craned her neck from side to side, looking for her coach. She finally spotted Mrs. Malone with minutes to go before the race.

"Hey, listen," Carmen said urgently, already stepping away. "I'm just going to say hi to my coach and check in with her. I'll meet you back here."

"Yeah, no problem," Jenny said as she continued to stretch.

Carmen jogged over, seeing that the entire Malone family had come. Joanne was not in running clothes as promised. Good. There was one change to prevent history from repeating itself.

"Carmen, great—I was running late, so I haven't gotten to check the roster to make sure people have checked in." Mrs. Malone looked clearly frazzled from her late arrival. "You're running the 5K, right? Try to keep it under eight minutes a mile, but if you only make it under nine minutes a mile on average, we may still be able to place as a group."

She was not a strong team member, but she could do under nine minutes a mile. Mrs. Malone looked distracted, and having spotted someone else on their team, she made her excuses and hurried off, leaving Alice with her dad and Carmen.

The young girl's eyes looked bloodshot. Carmen signed, "Are you okay?"

Alice nodded, signing as she did so. "Rough morning. Dad and I will stick close to Mom. We'll see you at the finish line."

The clock was ticking—for the race to start and Mrs. Malone.

The loudspeaker crackled and a man's voice boomed over the crowd. The racers took their places. Carmen noted all the payphones in case they needed to call an ambulance. Carmen found Jenny just in time for the race to start.

Carmen had never run faster. Mostly, she just wanted the race to be over. She ended up leaving her friend in the dust. Her chest felt tight, and she was breathing fast as she crested the last hill, the finish line in sight. Brushing sweaty damp curls from her face, she scanned the finish line area for an ambulance or for any sort of commotion. There was only the usual race day crowd. Finally, Carmen spotted her coach.

She was fine. She was standing there—long blonde hair under a hat, coffee in hand—cheering for Carmen.

Carmen almost stopped in relief at seeing her, but instead, put on a burst of speed and raced downhill to the finish line. The clock showed less time than it had ever shown for her. Carmen did the math, and it averaged at less than eight minutes a mile. She felt like throwing up. Of course, she wasn't first, but she certainly wasn't last. Her team might even win with her much faster time if the rest did as well as they usually did. She practically collapsed at the finish line, and the Malone family crowded around to congratulate her.

Carmen met the younger Malone's eyes, and she had a massive grin on her face. Alice looked at her watch, then gave Carmen a subtle okay. Somehow, history had not repeated itself. She responded with a huge smile of her own. She wasn't sure how, but Mrs. Malone was okay.

The next day at school, Mrs. Malone was missing from class. Carmen freaked out and rushed to the library to check her email and was relieved to see an unread message from her young friend.

> "Mom is okay, some of the imaging from her neurologist was concerning, and she has a last-minute appointment today. We may get some answers and preventative plans to what happened before."

The younger Malone wasn't privy to all the adult mumbo jumbo medical talk, but Joanne was rushed into an outpatient procedure and was back at school in time for Carmen's senior finals. The crisis was averted somehow.

Carmen reviewed the time-travel list in her mind again. She could finally cross off fixed points for sure. She wasn't sure how, but Mrs. Malone wasn't going to be dying in this timeline if they had anything to do with it.

1. ~~Single continuum~~
2. ~~Fixed points~~
3. ~~Time loop~~
4. Infinite timelines

CHAPTER 28

Prom dress shopping was done with Josie, Ganesha, and Jenny. Carmen found a stunning turquoise satin sheath dress she was willing to splurge on. She dyed the faded pink tips of her curly hair blue to match. Although her matchmaking at the previous dance went poorly, Carmen was glad she and her friends were going to the dance together, this time with very different dates.

Mattias and Jenny had run into each other at some party and they'd started talking. Not long after, Mattias asked her to prom. Carmen might have been awful at matchmaking, but she accidentally brought them together somehow, so she counted it as a win.

The afternoon before prom, Carmen got ready alone in her room. She and her friends had splurged on a limo — mainly Logan and Mattias had — and it would be picking her up last. So she had a little extra time to get ready. She had the radio turned up, her gown on, and was putting sparkly pins in her mass of black and blue hair, when there was a knock on her bedroom door.

"Come in, Dad! But please put the camera away. I'll take pictures when..." Carmen saw her mom standing behind her through the vanity mirror. She whipped around.

"Hello, Anak."

"Mom!"

They both stared at each other for a long moment.

"I wanted to come back for your graduation," her mom said, which seemed like the last thing on both of their minds.

Carmen continued to stare at her. Her mom hadn't even walked into the room, her posture stiff as she stood in the doorway. Carmen's eyes filled with tears.

"Please don't cry." Her mom's defensive stance melted away, and she rushed to her side. "Your makeup is all done, and I don't want you to mess it up. You look so beautiful."

Carmen's mom enveloped her in a hug, her scent still the same powdery linen. Carmen hugged her back, then took her by the shoulders and forced her mom to sit across from her.

Words tumbled out of her in a torrent from months of pent-up emotions. "I know you were unhappy, Mom. I understand why you left Dad. I get it. But...you just *left* without telling me. Why?" Her voice was squeaky and hoarse from emotion.

"Anak..." Her mom sighed. "I was just so angry."

"At Dad?"

"I read your journal."

A hot flush of surprise spread across her face. Her mom had a deep furrow between her eyebrows, clearly still upset.

"How did you find it?" Carmen said faintly. "When?"

"You left it on the computer when you went to San Francisco."

Oh God, her blog. She'd said so many horrible things about her mom.

"I read it and... I saw how you saw me." Her mom's voice held a note of warning. "The only reason I was staying with your dad was to take care of you. A child should have a mother and a father. But I read your journal, and I thought, 'she hates me.' I thought 'why am I staying? Who am I staying for?' So, I left."

Flooded by guilt, the vicious churning in her stomach almost made her sick. "I don't hate you, mom. I was just...venting."

"Well, it hasn't been easy for me either. But I didn't think I was doing a terrible job at being your mother until I saw what you wrote."

"Mom, you didn't do a terrible job," she said weakly.

"No. The way you wrote it, all I did was yell at you and your dad. But you said such ugly things about me too. Why had I worked so hard, stayed with your dad when I was unhappy if you didn't need me or want me?"

"Mom...I'm sorry," she said with such raw emotion in her voice that her mother's angry words stopped. "I'm sorry I said I hated you... But you've been... You're so hard on me. And on, Dad. And the way you two fight is so savage. You say such *awful* things when you're mad. I'm glad you left Dad. I hate watching you two tear each other apart. But couldn't you be...I don't know, just *nicer*? To *me*?" Carmen could hear the anger in her voice now. "You left me, instead of trying to...*talk* to me about everything."

Her mom looked as wrecked as she felt, eyes glassy

from unshed tears and red blotches high in her cheeks.

"I don't know if I know how to *be* nicer. I will try. But people make poor choices when they're suffering. I was just... I've been unhappy for *so long.* But I hurt you, and I'm sorry I left you. It was...unforgivable. And no matter what, I always loved you. You should never doubt that."

Carmen's first impulse was to say she was forgiven, but that would negate how much it *had* hurt. Her mom's leaving had crushed her, made her feel abandoned and unwanted. After a pause, trying to gather her thoughts, Carmen spoke. "I know we've butted heads, and we're both to blame for that," Carmen rushed to continue when it looked like her mom might interrupt. "But I never thought you would just...run. And it *stung.* But you coming back means a lot too. I can forgive you, mom. I want to."

As if trying to match her thoughtfulness, her mom spoke slowly. "I know. I...continued to read your journal entries after I left, even though it felt like I was torturing myself."

Carmen thought back to her journal entries after her mom had left. She couldn't remember the specifics of what she had written, but she could remember the emotions. Anger. Shame. Betrayal. But she also understood and missed her mom. She hoped this showed in her journal entries too, how much she'd missed her.

Carmen's mom leaned over to hold her hands and looked into her eyes. "I am leaving your father, but I can't leave you too. I can't...I can't divorce my *child.* I love you. But you just make me so *angry* sometimes. You're so... so American. You act and dress and say things that are so...so different from how I was raised. And I'm just so *tired* of feeling like the bad guy. The way you talk to me.

It's nothing like how a child should talk to their mom. But reading your journal, I realize you still need me. So, I came back."

"I do need you, Mom. And I'm sorry." Carmen felt tears trace themselves down her face and swiped at them. Carmen felt wrung out.

"I'm sorry too. You said stupid things, but you're a teenager. I should know better. I shouldn't have left like I did." Carmen moved to the edge of the bed, where her mom was sitting, and they hugged.

The doorbell rang and Carmen pulled away to look at the time. It was likely Logan and the rest at the door.

"Honey, your makeup is a mess now," her mom said, brushing at her running mascara. "Let's fix it and talk more later. I'll be here when you get back."

"Are you and Dad...?" Carmen both dreaded and hoped for her to say that they were getting back together.

"We're still separating. There's just...it's complicated," she said vaguely. She continued, in a firmer voice. "But I'm still your mother. We'll talk about it more when you come home tonight. Now let's meet this boy I was reading about."

"Mom!" Carmen said, embarrassed. "I'm going to have to get another username. I can't have you reading all my stuff!"

Her mom sat up primly, a sniff to her voice as she spoke. "Your drawings were well done, although I don't understand this obsession with science fiction. And time travel? Stick with reality, Anak."

Carmen laughed as her dad came into the room to fetch her.

"Anak," he said, peeking into the room. "I thought I'd give you some time, but your friends are here."

Her parents avoided looking at each other, tense and awkward, and she understood why. That would probably never go away. But she was so happy they were there for her. She rushed out of her room to see all her friends at the apartment door, dressed to the nines. Crowded into the front room, Logan looked unnaturally stiff and formal, solemnly shaking her dad's hands. First time meeting the parents? Uncomfortable all around.

Logan's eyes lit up when he got a proper look at Carmen. He did a subtle scan of her but refrained from more than a "You look gorgeous, Trivia."

She did a model pose, kicking her leg out with a hand on her hip to whistles from the other girls. They didn't dawdle long in the living room, as it was cramped and technically her dad's bedroom.

Giddy with each other's company, they tumbled outside to pose for photos by the limo. Ganesha rolled her eyes at Carmen over some terrible joke. Jenny pushed her ample cleavage up for photos. Mattias, tattooed and pierced and good-natured, gallantly held Jenny's purse for her. They took dozens of pictures with a clunky "brand-new" digital camera instead of a phone. She still forgot sometimes what a difference ten years could make. Each couple took photos together, then only the girls and only the guys—the poses getting goofier and goofier—before they took one last group photo all lined up. They were finally allowed to leave for prom when her parents had run out of camera memory.

Once they arranged themselves and their heels, purses, and dresses, Logan pulled out a bottle of champagne he stole from his dad's stash. There was just enough for each of them to toast with.

Josie declined with a headshake and a frown. "I think

I've proven alcohol and I don't mix well."

They all laughed at that.

Logan held his flute of champagne up. "*Mabuhay!*" he said, with perfect diction.

The memory of their first meet-cute made her smile.

Logan had his arm around Carmen, and she loved the rolled-up sleeves and suspenders he'd worn, a vintage bolo tie with a turquoise pin that matched the color of her dress at his neck. He even wore black boots with a point to them, giving them a subtle flair.

Josie and Ganesha had decided to wear matching A-line dresses, their hair both styled slick and straight. Jenny and Mattias dressed in emerald, green, with the redhead in a sort of princessy strapless ballgown and Mattias in a green dress shirt with a neck ruffle that was over the top and very much him. He'd dyed his hair green to match, just like Carmen had dyed her ends blue.

"Hey, so check this out," Logan said excitedly. "My dad got me and my brother the new Nokia cell phone!" He pulled out the classic brick phone that would become so ubiquitous.

Ganesha made a face. "Is that so that people can keep track of you? No, thank you. Why would I want someone to be able to call me wherever I am?"

"I mean," Logan said. "It's pretty handy. If this limo broke down, I could just call a tow company! And check this out. It's got games preinstalled like a Gameboy."

Mattias and Jenny leaned over to look at the tiny black pixel screen that showed the little black snake of the game of the same name.

"Cool!" Mattias said. "Can I try?"

When they arrived at the high school gym, it was decorated with carnival lights and a big-top setup that

Carmen loved. Mrs. Malone was chaperoning, and it made Carmen happy to know that she had recovered from her minor but serious surgery.

When Mrs. Malone saw them, she smiled and held up a Polaroid camera. "Let me take a couple of photos to show Alice when I get home." She took a few, then shook them out. "Don't tell the principal I used so many on just you guys. I'll run out if I'm not careful." She gave them a wink.

They snagged a table, then went to the dance floor where Carmen saw Kelly with a new beau. Kelly smiled at them and gave a little wave as she danced nearby. A slow dance came on and Logan gathered Carmen up in his arms. She loved his exposed forearms and told him so, running her hand lightly across his prominent veins.

"Trivia, you like the weirdest things," he said, nuzzling her hair. "Should I have worn the Cheshire Cat suit tonight instead?"

"Or the Hook costume. I was into that one too," she said with a purr.

Leaning back, he made a face at her. "Gross! He was the bad guy!"

Carmen smiled up at him, and he leaned down to kiss her, a laugh still on his lips.

If she had to live the next decade all over again, if she never got to her own time and place, at least she had what mattered to her most — her friends, her family, and Logan.

A commotion interrupted their kissing, and they pulled apart to look over by the back door. Someone yelled for help. Carmen felt a shiver of déjà vu as she pulled away from Logan and stood on her toes to see over the crowd of dancers. The music cut out.

"Someone call 911!"

She started to walk through the crowd, Logan at her side. As she pushed past the gathered students, she saw Mrs. Malone on the ground. Cold panic filled her. Carmen rushed to her side, kneeling as she did so to check her pulse.

"I can help, I'm—" She realized she wasn't a nurse yet. "—I know CPR. Logan, call 911 on your cell phone if no one else has!"

Things happened in fast-forward. Mrs. Malone was rushed away by medics to the closest hospital. A friend of Logan's lent them his car so they could follow the ambulance, the limo not scheduled to arrive at the school for several more hours. They called Mr. Malone on Logan's new cell phone to tell him what had happened and where his wife was going. It always took a little longer to load Alice in their vehicle, so Logan and Carmen made it to the hospital on the proverbial coattails of the ambulance and followed her inside before walking back outside to wait for Alice and Mr. Malone.

Less than an hour later, Carmen sat on a bench outside the hospital with Logan's arms around her.

"Trivia, you did all you could," he assured her. "All we can do is hope now."

She had her face in her hands, Logan rubbing calming circles into her back.

"Carmen?" a male voice called.

Carmen looked up to see Mr. Malone and Alice in her wheelchair, quickly coming up the path from the hospital parking lot. Logan stood to meet them.

"Mr. Malone," he said, "we can show you where she is. They took her straight to surgery, but her stuff is in bay seven…"

Mr. Malone and Logan started up the path.

"I've got Alice." Carmen took Alice's wheelchair handles away from Mr. Malone. "We'll take the accessible path."

With a thankful smile, Mr. Malone rushed up the stairs.

Alice turned to sign to her as they rushed up the more roundabout path to the sliding front doors with EMERGENCY emblazoned above.

"Is she okay? How was she when you last saw her? Is it the same as before? Does it look like she had a stroke again somehow?"

"Slow down." Carmen tried to sign with one hand as she pushed Alice. "I don't know. Maybe?"

When they made it to the lobby, they got in the elevator to go to the waiting room for surgery. They were able to sign then.

"I don't know," Carmen said. "She's alive, but she might have been having a seizure?"

Carmen was on the verge of tears, and Alice was openly crying, big tears falling from her eyes as they entered the waiting room. They paced, stressed, comforted each other, and took snack breaks over the next couple of hours. Mr. Malone urged Logan and Carmen to go home and get some rest, but Carmen could not leave Alice's side. Grief was a complicated emotion, made all the more complex for Alice because she knew that Mrs. Malone's death might be an inevitable conclusion they couldn't prevent. And then to be given hope just a couple of weeks ago that this might be preventable!

A surgeon came out to speak with them a few hours later. He had a solemn look on his face, and Carmen braced herself. She looked at Alice who seemed so small in her chair as she warmed her hands on a cup of hot chocolate.

"Are you the family of Joanne Malone?" the surgeon said, looking at the only adult in the group.

"Yes, doctor?" Mr. Malone stood from his seat next to his daughter.

"Your wife is in recovery now."

The room collectively exhaled the breath they all held.

The surgeon continued. "I wanted to let you know it was a difficult procedure, but I was able to stop the bleeding. Your wife had an aneurysm, and we don't know..." He devolved into medical talk, but Carmen went to Alice, who was shaking—with relief or fear, Carmen didn't know.

"It sounds complicated, but she's out of surgery." She signed to Alice. Carmen wasn't sure if Alice had gleaned from body language and lip reading that her mom was okay, but Carmen made sure she was aware. Her mom was alive.

Alice wilted with relief. "Is she awake? Can we see her?" she signed rapidly.

"Um..." Carmen listened back in on the surgeon and Mr. Malone's conversation.

"...We've sent her for imaging, but we won't know the extent of the damage until..."

"It sounds like she's still getting testing done, and she's not awake yet, so we still have to wait." Carmen sat next to Alice to put an arm around her.

Logan came over to sit as well. He tried to distract Alice by using basic alphabet spelling to ask her the signs for certain useful words. Logan finally got up to grab more hot chocolate, and Mr. Malone rushed to his car for a bag he'd forgotten, so Carmen and Alice finally felt free to talk.

Alice's hands moved quickly as she asked what happened at the dance.

"She collapsed, but someone said she may have had a seizure? I didn't see what happened at first, but she was on the ground when I got to her." Carmen looked pensive. "Honestly, it was a little eerie..."

"Why?" Alice signed.

Carmen hesitated.

"Come on, I can handle it." Alice gave a half-smile, faded but present. "Remember, I'm not really seven."

"It was almost exactly what happened to you at the reunion. I mean, not exactly...but similar enough to creep me out. Same room, dancing with Logan, then someone in the crowd yelling 911, me running to help. Same room, same people around me. It just felt weird. It gave me déjà vu, like time repeating itself." Carmen paused, not sure of what else to say. "It just reminds me of how strange we are to both be here, back in time."

"Yeah...I feel lost right now, honestly," Alice signed slowly. "I hate to think it, but it's feeling like we can't cross off fixed points on your time-travel list yet. Are certain events unavoidable?"

Mentally, Carmen underlined fixed points on her mental list, as the dreaded possibility of history repeating itself felt inevitable, sitting in the hospital, waiting to hear of news about Mrs. Malone's health.

1. ~~Single continuum~~
2. <u>Fixed points?</u>
3. ~~Time loop~~
4. Infinite timelines

"I do too. It just feels like why?" Carmen wondered. "Like, is there a reason we were sent back at all?"

"There might not be," Alice signed. "But I've gotten a year more with my mom. I wouldn't trade that for anything."

Offering comfort again, Carmen placed a hand on hers. Logan came back with hot chocolate and snacks. When Mr. Malone came back from the car, a bag slung over his shoulder, he finally convinced Carmen and Logan to head home.

Looking back one last time before the elevator doors closed, she saw Alice and Mr. Malone huddled together, his arm around her shoulders. Carmen held Logan's hand a little tighter.

CHAPTER 29

Groaning, Carmen opened her eyes. The light blinded her, and she had a piercing headache to go with it. She shut her eyes again, wincing.

Youch. Her head hurt.

Had she had too much to drink last night? She suddenly remembered Mrs. Malone and sat bolt upright. Her head *screamed* in pain, and she fell back to the bed, groaning.

"Shhhh, honey, lay back down," Logan said, and his warm fingers combed through her hair as his other took hers in hand.

She slit her eyes open. She heard someone else say "close the lights" in an accented voice, and the lights went dark. So, her mom must be here too? Why was Logan in her room in the morning? Carmen slowly opened her eyes, careful not to worsen the mind-blowing headache as she looked at Logan.

Logan.

With long hair in a bun and whisps around his face, he looked down at her. His closely shorn beard framed his usually smiling mouth. Her Logan. Adult Logan.

Oh. My. God.

His worried frown deepened. Had she said that out loud? She probably had.

"Hon, what's wrong?"

"My uh-my head just really hurts. And so does my nose." She clumsily reached for her face and felt bandages. "Ow."

"Don't touch that." He pulled her hand away. "You broke your nose last night. And have a pretty bad concussion. What do you remember?"

She looked around. She was in a hospital room. She could tell by the setup. Her mom was sitting in a corner looking haggard and old, with gray hair in a messy low ponytail. Josie and Ganesha sat on a window ledge. Adult versions, with Josie's pregnant belly poking out and Ganesha in the velvet suit and colorful hair extensions.

"Not a lot," was all she could manage to say.

The doctor came in, checked her out, and sent her for imaging.

Logan was alone in her room when they wheeled her back in. He looked frazzled and tired, his sleeves rolled up and his shirt untucked, with hair coming out of its customary bun.

Turning to her, he had an expression of relief on his face. "I'm so glad you're okay. I was so worried when you didn't wake up right away."

"I was only out one night, right?" Sudden worry made her forget that he, Ganesha, and Josie were still in the clothes from last night. Last night. At the reunion.

"Yeah, are you remembering what happened?"

"Um. Kind of… It's a little fuzzy. Is Alice okay?"

He raised his eyebrows in confusion, then lowered them in recognition. "Oh, the girl in the wheelchair? I never caught her name. You did?"

"Yeah… Listen, I had the weirdest dream while I was out." Carmen didn't know why she hadn't told anyone before, but she felt she needed to tell Logan now, even if he thought she was crazy. She briefly outlined what had happened over what felt like the last nine months to her. She finished with, "It all felt so *real*. So vivid…"

"So, you dreamed you were seventeen years old again and had to live over your senior year? It sounds like the kind of dreams I used to have on Ambien." He laughed but grew serious. "What…else do you remember about last night?"

"Yes," she said.

"Yes…what?" he said, tentative hope in his voice.

"I remember you proposing, and yes, yes, a thousand times yes."

A smile slowly spread across his face with each yes, until he was beaming. His prominent canines made their appearance, and she grew warm at his wolfish grin.

He gently held her face, then kissed her long, slow, and sweet. He was extra careful around her broken nose, the bulky bandage a barrier to the kind of kiss an accepted marriage proposal deserved. He pulled away with a massive grin on his face.

"I am so relieved!" He looked around them. "This wasn't quite the setting I had in mind, but I'll take your yes anywhere!" He kissed her again, more fiercely this time. He pulled away to look her in the face, serious again. "I wasn't sure…when you took so long to answer,

I wasn't sure if the timing was all wrong, or you just didn't know how to turn me down..."

"I just needed some time." She smiled slyly at her joke before her smile transformed into something more earnest. "But *yes*, Logan, I want to marry you."

Later that evening, after the doctors had done their tests, and she was finally discharged, she passed down a hallway of windowed rooms. She could see inside, and there was seventeen-year-old Alice, with her father in the hallway talking to a doctor. She and Alice briefly made eye contact. Alice smiled, waved, and signed, "Carmen," using the C-with-noodles unique to her.

So...it might have been real for both of them if Alice knew her sign name. Carmen desperately needed to speak with Alice somehow.

"Hey, Logan," Carmen said, sliding off her new engagement band and hiding it in her pocket. She internally winced at the minor panic this might cause him. "I think I'm missing my ring." She flashed her empty hand. "Could you go back and check?"

His eyes widened. "Yeah. You'll wait here?"

At her nod, he rushed off. Carmen stood from the wheelchair they'd made her take out of the hospital and walked over to Mr. Malone. He was grayer and more wrinkled, but still clearly the same gentle man she'd gotten to know in the past. He must have recognized her from her actions to save his daughter's life, as his eyes widened, and he cut himself off mid-sentence with the doctor he spoke with.

"Sorry, doctor, just a moment. Oh my gosh, you're the woman who saved my daughter." He stepped past the retreating doctor and clasped her hands. "Thank you," he rushed to say. "If you hadn't done the Heimlich, I don't know where we'd be."

"I'm just glad I was there at the right time and with the right skills, Mr. Malone."

"Oh! You know my name?"

"Oh — uh, I asked when I woke up and my family told me."

Looking at her nose, he winced, or more precisely, the giant bandage over her nose and her two black eyes. "It was a nasty blow. When the ambulance came they had to call a second one for you, too. You were out cold!"

"Yeah, I was out for about twelve hours, but I'm okay. Just a minor traumatic brain injury between new friends." She grimaced at her own gallows humor when he just looked more guilty. There was a loud clap from behind them and they both turned to look within the room.

Alice signed from her bed, sitting up and beckoning Carmen and Mr. Malone over. Alice gave a questioning sign, her face an exaggeration in confusion. The girl could act.

"Oh, I'm sorry, Alice," Mr. Malone said and signed contritely. "Terrible manners, speaking to someone without introducing you. This is the woman who saved your life. She gave you the Heimlich when you choked while you were seizing."

"Hi, I'm Carmen." She spelled out her name, then gave her sign name.

"Oh my goodness, and you sign!" Mr. Malone said in surprise.

"Hey, Dad, could you get me lunch? I'm starving." The cafeteria, Carmen knew from Logan's grumbling, was at the other end of the hospital. He'd be gone for a bit so they could talk.

He raised his brows, but conceded, leaving them to

their conversation in peace.

As soon as he was out of sight of the windows, Alice turned to Carmen.

"So..."

"We both lived for almost nine months in 1999 with our future knowledge intact?"

Alice laughed at her rapid-fire signing.

"If we hadn't, I'd be so confused right now. And probably calling security about the crazy person in my room."

Exasperated, Carmen threw her hands up in the air. "That whole time we were obsessing about it being time travel when it was option number five, a dream!"

Carmen reviewed the well-worn list, ticking them off as she signed, and added the fifth.

1. ~~Single continuum~~
2. ~~Fixed points~~
3. ~~Time loop~~
4. ~~Infinite timelines~~
5. A dream

"A shared dream? I don't know. I feel like we traveled to some alternate timeline somehow together. Lived there for nine months and came back to our own. Dreams aren't so...real!" Alice emphasized the last word with a flourish of her finger.

"What was even the point of it all? Did we save your mom?" Carmen said, feeling hopeless about the whole experience. They hadn't been able to change anything. And the present was exactly as they left it. Not that she was unhappy to have her old life back, but seriously, what had been the point?

"I think...I think it's just like we said in the waiting room. Maybe...the point was the experience? I mean, I have nine more months of memories with my mom. I know the peculiarities of her face when she's happy or mad or sad. I know that she talks with her hands, even when she's not signing." Alice's eyes filled rapidly with tears. She blinked them away before continuing. "And I like to think there's a universe out there where my mom did survive. Before I went to bed, we'd been told she made it through the clot removal surgery. The doctor was talking about how resilient the body could be. He was talking about how vital the next forty-eight hours could be, and that her brain scans showed tons of movement, and how positive a sign that was. And I like to hope that the Alice I left behind woke up the next morning with a mom who might recover. With a mom she might have around a little longer."

Leaning forward, Carmen embraced the tearful teenager. It was so weird to see only hints of the seven-year-old she'd gotten to know. Carmen could see the woman she was growing up to be. She looked so much like her mother, and yet wholly herself.

Alice leaned away to sign, "And you got over your fear of commitment."

"Yeah, I guess I learned to choose Logan, despite all my commitment baggage," she said with an ironic twist to her mouth. Could that really be it? Less ironically, she thought of her lola, and all the cherished memories she had of their time together. Stories she would never have gained otherwise.

Carmen wasn't sure how she felt about their trip to 1999. A mixture of satisfied and frustrated? They might have both gotten what they needed rather than what they wanted.

Carmen accepted her mother's offer of a place to stay the night she left the hospital. She and Logan would leave the next day for San Francisco. Home. Logan and her mom had barely spent more than an hour at a time together previously because Carmen always made her visits economically short. She could sense them tiptoeing around each other, two almost strangers who would soon be family.

Carmen previously would have snapped back at her mom's sharp rebuke of, "Aye, don't take that!" when Carmen took one of the pain pills she'd been prescribed for her blinding headache. Carmen instead just reached out for her mom's hand and changed the subject. She understood that her mom had a long and challenging history with addictive substances.

Her mom seemed surprised at the touch but didn't pull away.

"Hey, Mom, I had the weirdest dream while I was out. Remember when Lola came to visit that Christmas break? I dreamed about that, and it put me in the mood for some pancit and sinigang. Could we come to visit for Christmas this year?"

Her mom looked surprised but pleased. Carmen hadn't spent a Christmas with her mom in a decade. "Of course, Anak, I'd love that. There isn't much room here, but you're welcome to come."

"Maybe we could even make some parols. Show Logan a true Filipino Christmas."

She and her mom would probably fight more than once. But the good did outweigh the bad, Carmen reminded herself. She knew she'd rather have her mom in her life than not. And Carmen figured she was an adult. She needed to start forgiving her mom. And maybe her mom would forgive her for all her years of being ungrateful. She didn't know if her mom had ever actually found and read her teenage journal, but Carmen hadn't been nice to her mom to her face either. Carmen figured she had amends to make either way, and Christmas together was a start. She couldn't control how her mom acted, but she could control her own reactions to her mom.

They wouldn't be best friends anytime soon. But she could see she needed a relationship with her mom, whatever that looked like. Carmen's trip to 1999 hadn't given her all the answers. Her relationship with her mom could not just be a simple yes like it had been with Logan. But she knew she needed her, so that was where she would start. By letting her back into her life.

She and Logan said their goodbyes the following day, with plans to start arranging wedding plans soon. Her mom was overjoyed at the proposal, although she made it a point to say the ring was small and that they could buy another when they had more money. Typical.

They headed to the hotel their friends stayed at the previous night. She and Logan planned on driving back, and Ganesha had asked to drive back with them. She'd missed her flight to make sure Carmen was okay.

When they entered the lobby to search for Ganesha, they found her, Josie, and Josie's husband Mark checking out at the counter. They both gave Carmen hugs when they saw her.

"I am so glad you're okay. That was a nasty blow," Mark said with a concerned frown.

"Everything intact? Do you know what it looks like

under that bandage yet?" Ganesha said as she took her card back from the person at the register.

"I've been too scared to look," Carmen said with a wince. "The doctor said it was a nasty break. I may need a nose job. Sorry Logan, the face you marry might be a very different face from the one you proposed to."

Logan's laugh was a joyous sound in the quiet of the lobby.

The girls both let out relieved sighs. Mark elbowed Logan. "Oh good, I was scared to ask if she said yes. It was a very eventful proposal, I'll give you that."

"Yeah, it did not go according to plan." Logan rubbed the back of his neck.

Her friends gathered their separate bags, and they all walked Josie and Mark out to the curb to get a cab to the airport. Josie hugged her first, then Logan, and Ganesha last. Carmen looked at her best friend's hug, with speculation. She would never have considered them a good couple until her time travel experience...

Carmen shook herself from matchmaking thoughts. She was *not* going down that road again. Josie was happily married, and Ganesha was happily dating people who were not her friends. Carmen had learned her lesson. She minded her business.

Looking over at Logan, she reached out to squeeze his hand. She learned other lessons too. Carmen resolved to stay out of her best friends' dating lives. She had her own life to live. She was just happy to have her life back—a likely better one from her experience.

EPILOGUE

During the wedding planning process, Carmen attempted to convince Logan several times to *elope* and avoid all the pomp and circumstance, and…honestly, she wanted to avoid her mom. Her relationship with her mom was *better*, but she was still herself and, therefore, a nightmare for events like holidays and weddings. Her mom had so many opinions! And none of them were things Carmen wanted. Still, as the date drew closer, she caved more and more. Logan helped with that.

"We have our whole lives together. She can have this day. I don't care."

"You don't care if we have a Catholic wedding? They're like three hours long," Carmen said with a frown.

"Okay, well, maybe not in a Catholic church…but if she wants to read a bible verse during the ceremony, I'm fine with that."

"Okay fine, are you okay with the men all wearing barongs?" Barong shirts were traditional Filipino white shirts that were semi-translucent and sometimes brocaded with gold thread. When Carmen had refused point-blank to wear a traditional Filipino gown, a Marie Clare dress, going so far as to purchase her dress without her mom's input or company, her mom had started harassing Logan about the men's wear instead.

"Actually…"

"*Et Tu Brutus?*" she said, overwrought horror in her voice.

"First, it's '*Et Tu Brute,*' because Latin uses the singular for—" Logan waved his hands at Carmen's expression and changed topics mid-sentence. "Never mind. Second, I happen to think they look nice. And we're having a beach wedding. All the white barong shirts will look nice. Your mom even showed me a much dressier white barong suit jacket. I think I could pull it off."

Carmen threw her proverbial hands up in the air, giving up on trying to control every aspect of the wedding. If Logan was okay with her mom's plans, Carmen would also learn to be.

In the end, they chose a gold-threaded mandarin-neck style that Carmen agreed looked good on the groomsmen. And Logan looked good in everything.

When she woke up from reliving her past, it had taken some time to get used to being an adult again. Get accustomed to her life. She often had to use her head injury as an excuse for her lack of memory.

She didn't know what to make of the nine or so months she had spent in the past. She had suffered a head injury and woke up less than a day later to find that nothing in her life had changed. So…was it a dream? Or did she and Alice travel to an alternative timeline like they discussed in the hospital? She told Logan all about it. He had a hard time believing it was a shared time-travel experience between her and Alice but offered an open ear and a sympathetic shoulder when she needed to vent about it.

She had difficulty remembering things she should know, like her debit pin, when bills were due, or where she kept her keys. She explained it all away as the head injury.

Going back to work hadn't been as bad as she feared. She'd taken a little more time off due to her concussion, so by the time she went back to work, all the patients were different, and she hadn't been expected to know who they were.

In the planning process for the wedding, she got very invested in designing her save the dates, wedding invites, place settings, signs…

As much as she complained about how much work it took to plan a wedding, she also enjoyed the artistry of it—picking colors and designing invites and table settings. Several of her friends and family liked the save the dates and invites enough to ask her to create invites for their celebrations—baby showers and weddings and graduations. A part of her felt fulfilled doing something creative again.

The whole time in the past she had longed to be back in *her* time. And here she was again! But…things were different again. Or, she had changed, and things looked foreign to her now. She was mending those parts of her that she hadn't even realized were broken.

She and her mom still struggled to see eye to eye, but at least she was letting her back into her life again. And Carmen was being creative again! And she had *her* Josie and Ganesha- not the pod-people high-school versions she had spent almost a year with. Which was unkind—they were exactly as they had been. She had just viewed them through the lens of adulthood.

And here they were on the day of her wedding. She couldn't believe she stressed about this day for so long.

With a flutter of nerves, she stood at the end of the sandy aisle, looking out at her gathered family and friends. Logan stood at the altar with his brother at his side, backlit by the setting sun and the white peaked ocean. In typical Ganesha fashion, she wore a beautiful mandarin collar barong suit that Logan and her mom had chosen for the groomsmen, wearing her long black hair braided with multicolored ribbons. Josie stood next to her, holding both hands of her barely toddling one-year-old, dressed in the most precious flower girl dress money could buy. Ganesha's date Kelly sat in the crowd—a year-long relationship that had started at their reunion. She could see her mom sitting in the front row, phone camera in hand despite the photographer taking professional photos. Her dad held her arm, ready to walk her down the aisle, and the music swelled to the song Logan proposed to.

> *"Lucky to have her,*
> *Lucky, she has you.*
> *With a winning hand at poker,*
> *I'd still bet on you.*
> *If I walked by a four-leaf clover,*
> *I'd always pick you.*
> *I'd choose a life sober,*
> *than a day without you..."*

Her nerves settled as her eyes locked with Logan and

the future she looked forward to having with him. For as much as books and movies glorified this day, she realized this ceremony was only a public way of saying she would continue to choose Logan. And choose this version of herself. This happy, creative, warm, complicated life she had built for herself.

She couldn't wait for what the future had in store for her.

Vanessa Aziz spent the first ten years of her adulthood adventuring. She's lived up and down the California coast, Nevada, the Alaskan frontier, England, and Eastern Europe. She's jumped off mountains, swam with whale sharks, excavated 15,000-year-old archaeological sites, and lived out of a backpack for months at a time. She is more often found writing about adventures than living them these days.

She is first-generation half-Filipino and half-Pakistani. She always felt a lack of representation in media growing up, so now she writes the kind of novels she wishes to see more of. Her stories are populated with quirky protagonists finding their way in the world when traditional labels don't fit. Her debut YA time travel novel Play it Back is inhabited by such characters. When she's not writing, she works as a nurse in child psychiatry. She and her husband Tomas are raising two bright young children, Lincoln and Luna, in Las Vegas, NV.

Made in the USA
Monee, IL
25 October 2023